Nor Hell A Fury

by

Stella
Wallace

First paperback edition, December 2017

For my Dear Dee Rear

"And is Man any the less destroying himself for all this boasted brain of his? Have you walked up and down upon the earth lately? I have; and I have examined Man's wonderful inventions. And I tell you that in the arts of life man invents nothing; but in the arts of death he outdoes Nature herself, and produces by chemistry and machinery all the slaughter of plague, pestilence, and famine... There is nothing in Man's industrial machinery but his greed and sloth: his heart is in his weapons. This marvellous force of Life of which you boast is a force of Death: Man measures his strength by his destructiveness."

- Bernard Shaw, Man and Superman Act III

A 1971 Monte Carlo speeds passed a rugged, lone man walking along a dark sidewalk. The car hits hard a black teen with a red cap crossing the street. The lone man glances over as the boy's body flies high through the air and meets concrete with a thud, bones snapping in the landing. The car and the lone man continue on without so much as a hitch. Distance voices cry out in desperation and despair.

The aisles stock sugared cereals and soda, mostly. Many of the boxes have been opened and left to spill onto the filth-ingrained tile floor. The produce section has bruised fruit and browning vegetables. Flies merge with overhead fluorescent lighting to create a loud buzzing sound that permeates the stale air. A pretty check out girl punches numbers into the register for the black teen with the red cap. He holds his side and a bloody handkerchief to his head. "Looks like that car got the better of ya. Tsk tsk. Will that be all?" the pretty check out girl asks. The black teen nods, then hands over a few coins and walks out with his bag.

The lone man steps up. "Pack of smokes," he drawls.

"Oh, hey Nash! How ya holdin' up?" Behind her is a fully stocked rack of nameless cigarette packs. She grabs one and throws it on the belt.

"It's a long haul, Kimberly. No doubt about that."

"Don't I know it. I don't think my feet will ever stop hurting! Anything else for you today, hun?"

Nash smiles and lights up a cigarette from the fresh pack. "Nah, doll. I'm good for now," he says and flips her a coin. She catches it midair with a giggle. He exits.

The scuffed metal siding lines the stale front of a local dining establishment. Through greasy windows, patrons sit alone at hard wood tables and chairs, consuming plates of greenish grey food matter. The restaurant is nearly silent except for the vile human noises of openmouthed chewing, labored breathing, and flatulence. Accompanying the orchestra of bodily functions, the faint sound of scuttling insects and rodents fill the gaps between the gasps. The faces vary in ethnic origin, most are pock marked, teeth rotted or missing. The women are without compassion, the men stupid and mean.

Nash pulls open the door and strides in. He takes a seat at the counter, his back to the door. A plate is put in front of him and he begins forking greenish grey mash into his mouth as fast as he can. He stops only to peer from side to side, his red-rimmed eyes alert and defensive, perpetually on guard.

Three men walk through the front door with purpose. They are big and brutish and carry wrenches and tire irons. No one dares respond except Nash, stopping mid swallow, fork frozen directly in front of his mouth. He looks forward at nothing in particular, breath held.

The first man walks up to Nash and taps him on the shoulder. "Where are the coins?"

Instantly, Nash spins to his left and seizes the hand that touched him with his left hand, while thrusting his right hand, and fork, into the man's guts repeatedly. The wrench he'd been toting falls with a loud clang on the linoleum as Nash makes a final stab to the first man's eye. He screams in German and falls to the dirty diner floor.

The second and third men spring to action. Nash kicks the legs out from the quickly approaching second man, grabs a knife from the countertop, and jabs it into the chest of the third man, puncturing a lung. The third man shouts out in pain using Italian obscenities, clutching his chest as he falls backward and toppling over an old man eating the grey porridge. Nash turns back to the counter and smashes a water glass on the Formica top. The second man scrambles to his feet and takes a swing at Nash with his tire iron, connecting to Nash's back. Nash absorbs it and turns to rake the second man's face with shards of glass. "Fuck! My eyes!" The second man falls to one knee with his face in his hands. Nash reaches for the first man's wrench under a chair and with both hands swings it like a bat to the back of the guy's head. The second man face plants into the floor and remains there, silent, as Nash throws a coin down on the counter in front of his plate. The coin is silver, and has the face of a man with long, curly hair. The expression is that of a smirk. Nash strides out the front door as the three men begin stirring and stand up, collecting themselves, brushing off their clothing, cursing a torn jacket. They make their way out as the waiter straightens up the chairs and tables, unfazed. The patrons never stop to look up and continue eating.

I I

Gripping the edge of a department store counter piled high with crisp, new clothing, a harried woman is doing her best not to scream. "I know for a fact there's money in my account!" The cashier gives the woman an icy smile, hands back her card. "Here, try this one," the woman says, shoving another card forward that declines to work as well. A line has started to form behind her. "That doesn't make any sense!" She throws her hands up and walks out, exasperated.

Sitting forlorn in the parking lot of the mall, she attempts to start her car again. The engine refuses to turn over. "Shit!" She rummages through her briefcase to find her cell phone, leaving a message. "I'm stuck at the mall. The car won't start. There's no money in any of the accounts. I can't take this any more, Robert!"

She hangs up and forces a deep breath into her lungs. Her second call has her fighting back tears. When the person answers, she composes herself, "Hi, Lexi? It's Grace. I have a problem. Are you busy?"

"Grace?"

"Yes."

"What is it, dear? I'm with a client right now."

"Oh, you are? Well, yeah, it's kind of an emergency."

"Can't it wait?"

"My car broke down and I can't get Robert on the phone."

"That's what Triple A is for, dear."

"We don't have Triple A. Look, I don't have any money. Can you please pick me up? I'm at the mall."

"Why don't you just get a new car already?

"I'm aware of that."

There's a beat. "Okay, you're going to have to give me forty minutes."

"Thank you, Lexi," Grace's ears burn with shame.

Robert Rice, disheveled in appearance, sits slumped over in his chair. The rows of traders sit in front of their

10

computers, engaged on the phones. The four o'clock bell rings. Robert drops his face in his hands.

The other traders pack up to leave. Don Osmond, the accounts manager and the eyes and ears for Crowning Capital, approaches Robert, leaning in. "If you'd stop running home to your wife all the time and start playing the game, you wouldn't be sitting here with your head in your hands," he says with a short pat on the back.

A voice from the front of the room rises above the chatter. "Robert! In my office!"

Robert groans. Mark Bean, Robert's young right hand man comes up behind Robert. He puts both hands on Robert's shoulders. "Keep your head up. We'll get 'em tomorrow. Go see what Marty says. I'll wait for you," he offers, pushing his glasses further up his nose.

Robert shuffles his feet, head down, towards the boss's office. He waits outside the door until he is waved in. He takes the position in front of the big oak desk, bracing for impact. Marty Harrison, a silver fox, is looking at his computer screen, calculating numbers. He shakes his head. "This office seats only those that produce. And you are not producing."

"I know I've been off. But I've been..."

"Are you giving me an excuse? If that's the case, I'll put you in a hospital because excuses are diseases. I do not work with people with excusitis."

"Jesus, Marty, I'm going to turn it around.

"Here's the bottom line. You have to make this your life again. Get out there. Take your clients to dinner, get them laid, if they want drugs, get them drugs, if they like little boys, set them up with fourteen year olds and take pictures, I don't give a shit. Make it your priority. In this office, you eat shit fuck sleep this job. There's no room for pikers here."

"Marty..."

"I don't want to hear it. Get out of my office."

Robert sulks out and onto the trading floor towards his desk to collect his things. Mark is on the phone with a client. Robert sits his dead weight down. Mark covers the mouthpiece, "Are you ok?"

"My back is against the wall."

"Let's regroup and take no prisoners."

"I'm going home."

"Grab a drink with me. We'll figure out a game plan. Come on, man. You got this!"

"I can't. It's just not in me. I'll see you tomorrow," Robert says and makes his exit especially pitiful.

Ι Ι Ι

The walls of the hallway have a dank cave feel, the ever-present sound of scuttling vermin permeates within. Nash, returning home, finds the door of his apartment wide open and his old, black, rotary phone ringing incessantly. The small, dingy apartment has been overturned. A young woman, once pretty, is viciously rummaging through Nash's belongings, pulling out dresser drawers, and dumping the contents out on the stained wooden floor. Nash stands in the doorway, taking in the scene. The moment he steps into the room, the woman freezes, petrified. "Go ahead, Sheila. Answer it. It ain't for me," Nash states simply. The phone continues to ring. "Those coins were meant for us. Now, you're stuck here. Why'd you do it?"

12

"Because I never loved you!" Sheila screams, her shrill voice betrays the panic she feels.

He grabs her by her foot and drags her across the floor, her jeans sliding off her thin frame, exposing her ass, splintering it, and dumps her out the front door. He slams the door in her face.

She immediately starts banging loudly, and screaming, "They're coming! They know it's here! They're coming and they'll get it. They'll get you!"

The phone continues to ring. Nash flings open the closet door to reveal a couple of pieces of dark gray and black clothing. He grabs a duffel bag from the closet and throws the clothes in the bag.

"You want love? Is that what you're looking for? You love me? Open the door! Open it!" Sheila's muffled cries offer no recourse.

He walks to the other side of the room and picks up a pole. Using it as a lever, he jabs the pole between the floorboards directly underneath the mattresses and pops one of them up. Inside the hole lies a heavy sack. Nash takes it out and it jingles. He places it in the duffel bag, and zips it up. He goes over to the bathroom. The single, unprotected bulb coming out of the wall in Nash's bathroom illuminates white-hot light as the switch is flipped. He walks over to the sink and splashes the brown water coming from the faucet on his face. He takes a long, hard look at himself in the mirror. "Fear. False evidence appearing real."

He grabs the duffel bag and walks towards the door. He opens it and Sheila lunges at him. Nash grabs her head and pushes it into the wall. Her head hits hard and she slides down the wall onto the floor. He steps over her and hurries out.

Wet garbage blankets the ground. Shadows move quickly across walls of buildings with no physical counterpart. Rats feast on everything they can sink their teeth into. Distant cries share the same futile plea for comfort from the despair of decrepitude.

From a dark corner emerges Nash, moving stealthily between dingy doorways. He comes upon an old man in an alleyway having sex with a woman bent at the waist. A bum stirs in a pile of trash near their feet, blending in with the detritus. The old man notices the bum and keeps pumping. Nash is swift to pass them. An ugly old woman approaches. As he walks by her, her face contorts and she hisses at him. He makes it to the end of the block and rolls up on Bar None.

Two huge bouncers, standing seven feet tall and bound with muscle, block the bar entrance. Nash is straight to the point, "No one gets in. We're closed. You," he points to the one on the left, "bring the car around." The bouncer nods his head and disappears around back. The other bouncer squares his shoulders, planting himself firmly on the ground, and guards the door. Nash eyeballs the street then enters.

The inside of the bar is covered in red velvet. A repetitive riff plays, as a skipping record would, and it's awfully loud. There are a few people inside, each more hideous than the next. Standing in a corner is a toothless slattern flirting with a fat man, a bottle of beer jammed in his tartan lapel pocket. He puts his arm around her loose body, running a hand through her careless hair and sticks his tongue in her mouth. An old man sits on a stool looking down at his crotch, "No. No. No. No. No. No. No. No."

Nash pushes passed him to the bartender, skinny and scared, "Put a call out to Ricardo. I need to see him now."

"Why we closed?"

Nash grabs him by the throat and pulls him forward, "Listen, you fuck. Get Ricardo on the horn. I didn't hire you to ask questions." The bartender hurries off. Nash grabs a bottle of whiskey from the till behind the bar. He takes off the pourer and drinks from the bottle, carrying it with him to a stairwell leading down to a basement office.

The basement is filled with broken chairs, old rolled up rugs, and scattered papers on the desk. A wall calendar has scribbles but no dates on it. A file cabinet is open with papers spilling out. The sound of scuttling insects and rodents permeate the space. Nash gathers a few things and throws them into the duffel bag. He walks over to a dartboard and grabs three darts. One, two, three he throws them into the center, unaffected, walking to the board to retrieve them. Ricardo, a young, tough, Puerto Rican gang leader, wearing his colors, walks in as Nash continues to throw Alan Evans shots. Ricardo watches Nash in silence, arms crossed. "¿Qué pasó?"

Nash turns to Ricardo. "Take over the joint for me. You're the only one I'd ask."

"How long, homes?"

"I don't know."

"Not many people would give up a business down here, unless they were thinking of buying themselves out."

"You know I can't answer that."

"Tell me something, ese."

"We're all bottom feeders down here. But taking what you think you can get puts you back where you started. The trick is *you must earn*," Nash says, tossing him the keys. He grabs his duffel bag and walks out.

A black Cadillac comes to a screeching halt at the curb in front of Bar None, stopping inches from where Nash is standing. The first bouncer steps out of the driver's seat and opens the back door. Nash peers from side to side before climbing into the dark interior. They speed off.

The sky is dark and the rain bitter. The headlights of the Cadillac reveal only the empty road ahead, deep black wasteland beyond. The relentless distance consumes nerve.

The car pulls up to a black wrought iron gate that closes as swiftly as it opens. As the car hugs the last bend of the covered way, passage along the outer edge of a ditch protected by a rampart forming glacis ten meters wide, the hulking fortress juts out of the darkness illuminated only from the medieval torch sconces burning blue despite the searing rain. Nash enters through a wicket set into the side gate door.

A long, lonely hallway leads to a waiting room brightly lit by buzzy florescence. A secretary sits with her hands folded in front of her. She is drop dead gorgeous and unwavering. Her desk is empty but for an old fashioned rotary phone. A single wooden chair sits in the corner. Nash walks up the desk.

"Do you have an appointment?" The secretary doesn't look up.

"I have an appointment with my dick in your ass."

The secretary does not respond.

Nash shakes the bag with the coins in it. "I have my buyout, you cold bitch."

16

"One moment," she picks up the phone and waits a brief moment. "Sir, I have a demon here with his buyout," she says, setting the phone down. "He'll see you right away. Please have a seat."

Nash takes the small chair indicated. The secretary sits motionless, eyes forward, hands folded. He looks around, taking in the room. Ultimately, he fixates on the one thing in the room that's worth looking at: the bombshell secretary. He slowly smiles at her. She does not respond, staring straight ahead. He stands up and approaches the desk, bringing his face inches from hers. She does not flinch. He straightens up and follows her gaze to find a mirror hanging on the wall opposite her desk. She stares directly into it. A loud bell goes off in the room, causing the secretary to jump. The bell stops as quickly as it started. The secretary takes a moment to catch her breath. "Right this way," she ushers him through a gold door in the back of the room.

The gold door opens into an expansive room with no ceiling, only blackness from above. The walls are lined with towering bookcases, first editions of every great work. The office is warmly lit, and impossibly silent. A large, mahogany desk sits in the middle of the room. The Devil, a man of small stature, sits comfortably in a very expensive suit. His long, wavy hair is impeccably groomed. He is the man on the coin. His demeanor is serene and composed, a quiet beauty about him.

"There are so many of you. Remind me. Who are you?" the Devil purrs.

"Nash."

"What is it you want, Nash?"

Nash drops the money on the table, "I want to buy my way out. What else?"

17

"Confidence. I like that. You think you have nothing to lose. Just remember, it could always get worse," he smiles with a wag of his finger. "Now, how was it that I got your soul?"

"Let's just say I wasn't a humanitarian."

"Took them for all they were worth, eh Nash?"

"That's the name of the game down here."

"I can see you're a natural." The Devil carefully takes a cigarette from a silver case in his jacket pocket and lights it with a silver Dunhill lighter. He exhales smoke in Nash's direction. "What makes you think you can buy your way out of hell? Is some nasty rumor going around my lair?"

"You can't buy anything of value with these coins. I figure they're worth something to you."

"Interesting logic. But let it be known. You can't buy me. I'm the Devil, for Christ's sake." The Devil stands and paces. "Are you familiar with demonic possession?"

"I remember seeing a few movies. The Exorcist, heads spinning around, vomiting pea soup."

"I love those Hollywood boys. Always exaggerating the truth," he smirks and returns to his seat at the desk. "A possessor, Nash, is an informant."

"So, you want me to be a rat?"

"Get it through your head. You are no longer human. You are a demon. You're working for the benefit of evil. You're working for me now."

"Is this an interview?"

"When a demon dares to face me, it piques my interest. It shows you still have will. How it is that this place has not broken your will, well, that interests me. I may have use for you."

"What's in it for me?"

18

"If going to earth, having a Wall Street job, a beautiful wife, a nice house, and a nice car benefits you, so be it."

"When does the informant part come in? Is there anything I should know?"

"Be sure not to sacrifice the power of enjoyment, but avoid suffering as a narcissist suffers by pursuing what's imagined to be better before securing the good, else you'll be forever tormented by what could have been with what was already yours." He stubs out his cigarette and adds, "I am certain you're a gaming man. A nod will do."

Nash shrugs, then nods. The Devil waves his fingers and Nash vaporizes into the black abyss above. The Devil picks up a file from his desk. A picture of a beautiful woman stares back at him. He runs his finger across her face.

I V

Inside the well-kept living room of a suburban home, Robert slouches on the meticulously clean white couch. His face has a worn down look, hair and clothing a mess. He sips scotch from a highball glass in one hand, a gun in his other. He stares at it, puts it in his mouth, squeezes his eyes tightly, but is unable pull the trigger. The sound of a car pulls up. He quickly hides the gun in the cushions of the couch.

Grace enters the house and sees him. "Is something wrong with your cell phone?"

Robert has picked up the drink and is staring into it, bracing himself for this well-worn conversation. "Gracie, please. Not now. Ok?"

"Are you the least bit concerned about what happened to me today? Are you aware we have no money in any of the accounts?"

"The market hasn't been good to me lately."

"It hasn't been good for months! How are we going to pay our mortgage? Please tell me."

"Gracie, I don't know what to do. I don't know how to get out from under this," Robert says, wiping at his tired eyes.

"I don't want to hear that! Our livelihood is at stake. My car is dead. Finito. How am I going to get to work?" She throws down her briefcase in a huff. "You've been telling me you'll buy me a new car for two years now. It's a wonder I make it out of the South Bronx every day in one piece without getting raped. Not that you'd care. Well, at least I'd be getting some!"

Robert's head lowers. He stares at his shoes.

"I used to call on you to take care of the things beyond my control. And you'd take care of them like a man. When was the last time you took control of anything?" her voice hitting a frenetic pitch.

Robert slumps lower in his seat, searching for a retort, defeated. Suddenly, his head tilts back as his body begins to arch. His eyes retreat into his head and he breaks out in a sweat. He quickly straightens up, eyes wide. He looks around the room, down at his glass as though he hadn't noticed it before. He chugs it down in two gulps. He lets out a huge exhale. He takes a peek down his pants and a sinister smile escapes him.

20

"What are you smiling at? You think this is funny? I don't find this a bit humorous. Our marriage is in trouble here!" Grace is exasperated.

Robert gets up and starts prowling around the room, picking up objects off surfaces, inspecting the place.

"What are you doing? Robert, say something!"

Robert looks back at her, eyeing her up and down as he would a barroom whore.

"What's that look?" she barely gets the words out. Robert downs the glass of scotch and pitches it against a wall, shattering it. He charges Grace and grabs her by the throat. He forces her to the wall, her eyes bugging out of her head in new fear. He stares into her eyes as his other hand rips her skirt off, reaches between her legs and touches her deeply. She cries out. He pushes her to the floor and mounts her, hard. Sounds of pleasure and pain escape her.

The morning sun begins to pour in from the newly opened window shades. Grace, dressed in a sharp business suit, flutters around the bedroom. As the light hits his eyes, Robert stirs.

"Good morning! The dreams I had! Wow!" Grace fastens her watch to wrist, sliding heeled shoes in place. "Do you think you can attack the market like you did me last night?"

He rubs his eyes with the palms of his hands. He looks at her with a big smile on his face and nods at his surroundings. The sound of a car horn is heard.

"That's my ride. I want you to know that this car situation has to be rectified today because I can't be carpooling with teachers that work for me. I leave myself open to the illusion of favoritism," she smiles and kisses the top of his head. Pulling back she stares at him oddly for a moment. She can't put her finger on it. "I'll see you later," she says and turns to go, giving him a double take. She walks out.

Robert gets up and stretches his new body. He walks over to the bathroom mirror and looks at his reflection. He runs his hand through his hair, slaps his belly, and grins ear to ear.

He enters the walk-in closet. Inside is a row of suits. He runs his finger down the string of them with a low whistle. He tosses each one aside until he finds an old school Brooks Brothers suit. He admires it and carries it over to the bed. He walks to the night table, picking up a wallet. Going through it, he finds a Crowning Capital business card with his name and an address.

Robert slugs down coffee in the kitchen, adorning a smartly tucked handkerchief in his double-breasted pocket, slicked hair, and freshly polished wing-tipped shoes. Through the window, he admires his beautifully landscaped lawn and long blacktop driveway. A shiny BMW stares back at him. He drops the cup in the sink, grabs the keys on a hook by the door and heads out.

The BMW is speeding down the suburban street. Kids waiting for a bus spill carelessly into the street. Robert aims for them as he passes, chasing them onto the lawn without slowing down. They quickly disperse, running for their lives, staring off behind him, watching him disappear in the distance.

Robert drives through the Mid-Town Tunnel, with hundreds of other commuters making their way into Manhattan. He arrives at the address on the business card and sprints out of a parking garage. He walks down the street quickly, bumping into people as though they were not there. He grumbles to himself in deep, guttural tones. The few people he knocks into, hard, respond with "Hey" and "Watch it" before moving on their way.

Robert eagerly rides up the elevator of the building, pushing past people in his way to be the first one off, oblivious to their stink eyes.

The rows of traders at Crowning Capital are lined up in front of their screens, waiting for the 9:30 bell. They pound coffee and banter as the ticker above their heads flicker with quotes and prices. Robert walks in, a glow about him, and stands in the middle of the room. The voices of traders come at him from all sides.

"Ooh, he got a new asshole ripped in him yesterday, look at that suit."

"It's all over now."

"This guy's so pathetic, I'm even embarrassed."

Robert is silent, eyeing the room slowly.

A voice breaks his steady gaze, "Robert! I want to show you something." Robert follows the voice and joins a nerdy looking kid, Mark Bean, at his desk. "You look good! Here, take your seat. I did some homework last night," Mark says, pulling out Robert's chair for him. Robert remains standing. "I've been analyzing the blue chips from the last…"

Robert listens to Mark with half an ear, turning his head to listen to all the other voices of those in the office. The voices of the other traders take shape until he can hear every word everyone is saying at the same time. His head moves from side to side, eyes darting in the many directions of the voices. One rises above the rest and interrupts the various sounds. "Hey Robert, you going to get your balls out of your ass today and make some money?" Brian Beckerman, a tall, heavyset man in his forties, stands at his desk across from Robert, peering over the divider with a slimy grin.

Sal Lombardi, a big nosed Goombah, walks over and smacks Robert's desk with the palm of his hand. Robert does not flinch. "How you doin', deadbeat? What say you earn that position today, huh?"

Robert stares back at Sal. "Hey Sal, I think this guy wants to fuck you," Brian leers.

"I'd get arrested if I banged this little girl," Sal chuckles.

Robert takes a step forward and presses his face an inch from Sal's signature schnoz and says, "You were a fat kid, right Sal? You had no friends. You still don't."

"What the fuck did you say?" Sal is incredulous.

Marty Harrison takes the floor to settle the men down. "Alright, everyone. Listen to me. Cold callers, hit those phones. Brokers, in the conference room. Now," he says and leads the way. The brokers file in. Marty continues, "Before David Brill takes over the meeting, I have a few things to discuss. I'd like to say first, a round of applause to Sal Lombardi and Brian Beckerman. They've sold over a hundred thousand shares of ARDEC this week alone. With that 3/4 rip, I see some new Ferraris for you guys in the future."

"Unfortunately, that whore of an ex-wife's taking this check," Sal groans.

"Well, if you went home at least once a week," one of the brokers says.

"Instead of blowing your boyfriend," another one adds and a few chuckle.

Sal yells, "Shut up you fat Irish fuck!"

"I'm fat? Your checks aren't going to your wife. They're going to your stomach."

Sal lunges at the broker, and chairs knock over as the others pull them apart.

Marty calls order. "Enough grab-assing. One last time. ARDEC. Push it. Don't let them sell. It's going to blow up. Push the stock. Now, next week we're introducing a new house stock, so go out, buy a mansion, buy a car, because the end of next month, you'll all be millionaires. Thank you. Now, here's David Brill," Marty says, nodding in Brill's direction and leaves the conference room.

Brill is a young, slick hot shot, full of cocky confidence. "Ok, guys. I'm going to start off the meeting with some new leads. Some willing clients. Let me see a show of hands. Who got laid last night?" A few brokers put their hands up. "Married guys put your hands down. Wives don't count. Hey Sal, hookers don't count, either." A few of the men laugh.

"They're all hookers. My date just ends a little quicker and I don't have to share the bed."

Brill throws leads to the few with their hands still up. He sees Robert's hand is in the air. "Robert, you can put your hand down. I wouldn't waste a lead on you if you fucked Cindy Crawford."

"How about ten leads for fucking your mother and coming on her face?" The crowd goes wild.

"What did you say, you pissant?" Brill comes at Robert and grabs the arms of Robert's chair, getting in his face. Robert doesn't flinch. "You don't generate enough money to even speak to me. We'd do better to put the office janitor in your seat," Brill spits.

"I'll bet you a hundred grand I double your sales today. But I need ten leads to do it."

"You don't have a hundred grand. And to be honest, I'm tired of kicking your corpse around."

"So, what you're saying is you're scared. You're scared of the challenge. Is that what your saying? Huh?" Brokers react with jeers.

"You don't have the balls," Brill speaks through gritted teeth.

Robert stands up and unzips his pants. He pulls out his dick, moves it aside, and cups his balls. "Don't these look like balls to you?" The room erupts.

Brill studies Robert closely. He counts out ten leads in front of Robert and says bitterly, "You better bring in the deed for your house tomorrow. If you're lucky, I'll let you rent it."

Robert heartily laughs in his face, takes his leads, and walks to the door. He turns around, "How 'bout this. If I lose, I'll quit. Are you ready for that bet?"

"I have to quit my job if I lose?"

"You're on," Robert smiles and walks out.

Brill stammers. The office oohs and aahs. The sound of the bell resonates. The stock market is open. The brokers empty out the conference room and take their seats. Phones start to ring. There is hollering, back and forth throughout the room, as brokers give and receive stock quotes into their phones.

"Three hundred shares of Chemtex at thirty-five. Should open at thirty-six, thirty-seven."

"Five thousand of DMR for Paine Webber, put it in the ICU account."

Robert turns on all of his equipment. He rummages through his client list with the alacrity of a new hire, spinning through each one as fast as he can turn to them, taking in every piece of information with lightning speed. He stares long and hard at his screen. He picks up the phone and dials a number, never taking his eyes off the screen. "Is this Roger Evans? Hey

26

Roger, you feel like making some money with me today? This is Robert Rice... Tell you what. Here's what I want you to do. I want you to watch Wal-Mart. It's at seventeen and a quarter. In fifteen minutes it's going to go to twenty-three and a half. Now you can get into this action now, or you can watch the stock and call me back in fifteen. What do you want to do...? Alright, good. Twenty shares. Believe me, Roger. You'll be calling me back for more," he says, hangs up the phone, picks it back up, and dials. He types in the order as the call is answered. "Hi, Carter Watts? How are you, Carter Watts, this is Robert Rice from Crowning Capital. Want to hear about the IPO...? The one that's going to make you a couple of million dollars... RUD, a new pharmaceutical company with a groundbreaking Alzheimer's drug, is at eight now. In an hour, you can call me back crying or laughing all the way to your third house in Monte Carlo," Robert says, placing the order, eyes locked forward.

Brill calls out from his office, "Oh Robert! BAM! Thirty thousand."

Robert sits as his desk, relaxed.

Mark Bean peers over his shoulder. "Robert, what are you doing? You can't trade the house stocks! They won't sell! You'll lose clients!"

"Hey Suzy, get me a coffee." Robert gets back on the phone. Mark stares at him, shocked. Robert cups the receiver, and stands up and gets right in Mark's face, "Hey sweetheart, the coffee ain't getting any warmer." Mark unfreezes and hurries off.

Robert stares straight ahead, the noise from the room blurring as the room metamorphoses into a giant, life-sized grid and numbers appear to come out of the walls and jump up onto it. Stock quotes stand in

27

perspective, with the current price in front and the future projection just behind it. Robert works off of the green and red of the plus and minus signs in a driving force of diabolical strategy. The numbers grow in size as the amount increases. They glow brighter as he acknowledges the stock at hand, the future quotes advance to the surface and newer quotes appear behind them. Robert works at breakneck speed in a whirlwind of phone calls and keypunching.

Don Osmond stands behind Robert, observing. He turns to Brill's office, sees Brill, and gives him a nod showing favoritism to Robert.

Brill turns to Jimmy, a rookie broker and his lackey, and fumes. "They're fucking with me. This is Don's gag on me. The gag of a century. All this bullshit with the suit and the bet? Robert is done!" Brill returns to the phone, agitated.

The four o'clock bell rings on the trading floor. Marty Harrison and the secretaries walk onto the floor, applauding. "Biggest day this office has had in two months! With the top trader today being Robert Rice with an outstanding three hundred thousand dollar day!" The office claps, congratulating Robert. Don and Marty give each other a surprised nod.

Brill is screaming from his office, "They're fucking with me! They can't be serious! This is a big fucking joke and I don't like it any more. Joke's over."

Marty walks over to the open door of Brill's office. "Hey, David. Maybe you should get rid of that Armani crap and stick to what works," Marty smirks and walks off.

Brill pushes his way through the crowd and looms up to Robert. "You lucky fuck."

28

Robert smiles. "Now that you're out of a job, you're a decent producer, you can come trade for me if you want."

"Let's go play with strippers!" Sal booms.

The men cheer and surround Robert, patting him on the back. He pushes them off of him. As they pack up to leave, different kind of phone calls go out.

"Hey Robert, call your wife," a broker offers.

"What for?"

"What are you outta your freakin' mind? The rules are you make nice at home so she doesn't take half. And don't forget to tell her you love her."

A broker turns to another broker and whispers in his ear. Robert's head perks up. "Blow? Who's got blow?"

The first broker stands there, staring blankly.

"You got coke? Give me some."

"Now?" he says, aghast.

"Yeah, hand it over, Santa."

The broker reluctantly hands over a small envelope. Robert opens it and dumps the whole thing into his cupped palm, put it to his face and sniffs deeply, head tilting back. His face is smothered in white powder. The broker shakes his head and walks out. "Got any more?" he calls out to the back of his head.

"Nah, man," the broker says over his shoulder and hurries out.

Robert picks up his phone and dials with flair. He speaks rapidly. "Hello sweetheart! Darling, light of my life, I have good news! Had a big day. I'll tell you later, more work to do here so I'm staying in the city tonight. I'll see you tomorrow. I love you. That's right, baby," he says sweetly and hangs up the phone and looks up. "Let's move!"

The rest follow his lead. As he reaches the door, he picks up a random dart off of a nearby desk and launches it across the room at the dartboard hanging on a far wall. Bull's-eye.

The men are engaged in raucous behavior at an uptown strip joint. Robert sits in the middle of the pack of heathens with his arms crossed. He hasn't pulled out dollar one. They are buying him drinks and lap dances. The energy is thick with a fraternity air. A girl is above him, moving her tits closer to his face. He sticks out his tongue and flutters it at her. She blows him a kiss. With a wide grin, he reaches out and grabs between her legs and squeezes. She shivers up her spine. The guys are egging him on. Strippers are waiting beside them, hungry for their turn with Robert. Money and drinks fly. The host approaches Robert from behind.

"You can't handle the girls, guy," he says gruffly.

Robert produces a wad of cash. "Where's your champagne room?"

The host takes the money discretely. "Right this way, Sir."

Robert takes the girl by the hand and follows the host into a hidden room at the back of the club. A moment later, loud screaming is heard above the music. The music stops, as people try to find the source of the screaming. Three bouncers run towards the back. They enter hidden room to find the stripper bent over, Robert holding her arms firmly behind her at impossible angles as he violently thrusts his naked lower torso into her ass. She looks over her shoulder at Robert with a face of fear and pure pleasure. Robert doesn't slow down at the arrival of the bouncers, but whips his head around, his face set in a snarl, and growls viciously at them.

They look on in horror, unable to move. As Robert finishes, he drops the stripper's arms, reaches into his jacket pocket, and hands each bouncer a hundred dollar bill. "Nice place ya got here. Maybe I'll buy it and give you guys a raise. How's that sound?" he flashes them a shit eating grin, grabs his trousers, and walks out.

V

Grace sits at her desk in her office at PS 151 in South Bronx. She's on the phone with Robert. "What do you mean you won't tell me? That's no fun. I want the gory details," she says, straining to hear over the sound of men shouting numbers and the names of stocks through the phone. She holds the phone away from her ear. "Robert! Robert, what about my car? We'll talk later. Dinner, okay? Robert?" She hangs up the phone with a sigh, and picks up some paperwork. There's a knock on the door. "Yes?"

Miss Lewis, a young and very attractive teacher, enters with two small boys on either side. Their noses are bloody and one is crying. "Mrs. Rice, we have a regular George Foreman and Muhammad Ali here."

"What round did they get to?"

"By the looks of it, the last one," she says, making a pained face.

"Bring them here, let's see what we got. Thank you, Miss Lewis.

"Don't worry, the pleasure is all mine." They share a smile and Miss Lewis exits.

"I don't want to know what happened. I want to know how are we going to fix it," she says, voice stern.

"He called my mother a stupid bitch," says the first little boy.

"I didn't..."

"Whoa! I don't like that language. Morris, would you want Eric to call your Mom bad names?

"No," Morris grumbles.

"Here's a little lesson for you. Treat others the way you want to be treated. And you'll find they'll like you a lot more. And Eric, instead of being physical, why don't you try talking it out with Morris? That way no one gets hurt," she sighs. "I'll make you a deal. I won't punish you. You're punished enough already by the looks of it. What I want you to do is shake hands and say you're sorry and if it isn't sincere, I see detention in your future for the both of you. Got it?"

They exchange sloppy handshakes and mutter "Sorry" before their eyes meet the floor.

"Good. Now, go see Nurse Elly and get cleaned up before you get infected. You know what that means?"

They shake their heads, shyly.

"It's like a bad case of the Cooties."

They moan and giggle.

She moves over to them and squeezes their cheeks. "Now get out of here!" she says, attaching a gentle nudge. They make their way with smiley faces.

Grace is supervising the rows of children on line for food in the lunchroom, navigating her way through those carrying their trays of warmed-over frozen pizza squares and milk cartons to their tables.

One student, Aisha, a tall for her age black girl in a pink sweat suit, is causing a stir at her table. She is stealing fruit cups from the smaller students, causing one little girl to cry. "What, you don't like that? You

32

cracked corn, nobody cares nothin' 'bout you, bitch," Aisha taunts.

Grace approaches the table. "Aisha, let's go. I want you out of here. To my office, now."

"What you think, I'm gonna be all that? You know it's five o'clock an' my Momma ain't gonna like you none," Aisha sasses, smacking a carton of milk off the tray of a nearby student, the contents turning the floor underneath it white.

Grace grabs her by the ear and whispers into it, "Why do you feel it necessary to disrupt my school all the time?"

"Burn in hell, mothafucka'!" Aisha laughs.

Grace removes her from the lunchroom.

The last of the buses pull out full of noisy kids. Grace walks with Miss Lewis to her car, "Would you mind switching your prep period from the morning to after lunch? I have a scheduling conflict and that change would really help me out."

"Of course. Do I get a raise?"

"Sure, I'll write it into our generous school budget," she jests. They get into the car.

Miss Lewis and Grace are sitting in traffic on the Long Island Expressway. Grace is scribbling in her daybook. Miss Lewis is smoking.

"Can I have one of those?" Grace asks.

"You don't smoke!"

"It's the second hand I can't stand. If you can't beat 'em..."

"I'll put it out." Miss Lewis goes to extinguish her cigarette.

"No! No I want to join," she smiles coyly.

Miss Lewis returns the smile and gives her a cigarette, "Do you want to go to a happy hour with me? For a drink?"

"I'm the principle and I'm married. Once those steps are taken, you no longer get to go to happy hours."

"I won't tell."

"Oh, tempt me, why don't you. That's not fair."

"You only live once!" Miss Lewis says delightfully.

"I get high off of responsibility. And control."

Don Osmond returns home from work. Lexi, Grace's friend and Don's trophy wife, washes dishes in a tight pink halter. She hears the front door and shuts off the water. "Honey! I'm packed for the Caymans! You promised this month, remember?"

Don enters the kitchen. "Call Grace and invite them to dinner. Tonight. Maybe that Sushi Restaurant on Eldridge."

"I thought we didn't like Robert anymore. Didn't we agree he's a dead beat?"

"Like him? Shit. He did it again! The guy just had two of the biggest days I've ever seen anyone have in that office since we started."

"Really? How much?"

"Somewhere in the neighborhood of six hundred k in two days. It's obscene and I've got to know what's going on. I have to get in on his action!"

"Six hundred?" Lexi gags.

"Call her now and tell her we're taking them out for a congratulations dinner. Do it."

Grace gets out of Miss Lewis's car, puzzled to see Robert's BMW in the driveway. The sound of an electric saw comes from inside the house as electricians install camera equipment in the front hallway. A man is carrying tools from a van parked in the street in front.

The men working in the front hall make room for Grace as she enters. She casts a glance at them. "Hello," she says, eyeballing their work.

"Hey, how ya doin'?" a worker offers back, turns to the guy standing next to him, and says, "You got a phillip's head?"

Grace continues through the hall, into the house. She puts her briefcase down on the front table and walks towards the living room, "Robert?" There is no response. The home phone rings and she answers it, "Hello?"

"Grace!" Lexi's voice has an exaggerated pitch to it.

"Oh, hi Lexi. How are you?"

"Congratulations!"

"For what?"

"Have you spoken to Robert yet?"

"No, I just got home. I'm sure he's around here somewhere. What's up?"

Lexi is busying her hands by wiping down a counter. "Well, honey, I'll let him tell you. But one thing's for sure, you're going to be a happy woman. Shall we say 8:00, Sushi Yoshi?"

"Ok. Great! See you then," Grace says and hangs up the phone and resumes the hunt for her husband up the stairs to their bedroom. The sound of sawing is heard from behind the door. Grace tries to open it. It's locked. "Hey!" she shouts over the noise. The sawing continues from behind the door. "What the hell do you think you're doing in there?" she hollers.

Robert is huddled in the middle of the floor, sawing a hole into the floorboards. He stops and looks up when

35

he hears Grace's voice. "Move along. Nothing to see here."

"I want to know what you're doing! Why is this door locked?"

Robert ignores her.

"Robert! Open this door!"

"Find something else to do."

"No way. I'm not leaving! Not until you tell me what's going on. What are these men doing to my house?"

"Just a few renovations. Don't worry, Darling. You'll love it."

Grace is growing frustrated having to speak through the door. "Oh really? That makes me nervous, Robert. You know I like to be a part of these kinds of decisions."

"You're just going to have to get used to some changes around here."

"Oh really?"

"Really. Look, you were married to a loser. Not any more."

"There are men downstairs installing cameras!"

Robert suddenly opens the door and pulls her close to him. He whispers in her ear, "It's a security system. To keep us safe."

"What about my car?"

"It'll be ready tomorrow."

"Lexi called. They're taking us out to dinner to celebrate. You want to tell me what's going on?"

Robert hands her several hundred-dollar bills. "Take the BMW. Get something nice to wear," he says, kissing her forehead, and shuts the door in her face. The sawing continues.

Grace and Robert arrive in style, he in his snazziest suit, and she in a stunning new dress. Lexi and Don are already seated, anxiously waiting. Lexi sees them arrive and catapults up to greet them with hugs. Don stands to shake Robert's hand. They all take their seats.

"So, Robert! Everyone was betting you were a one hit wonder. But two days in a row! Well done!"

"Grace, you must be very proud," Lexi purrs.

"I'm thrilled," Grace feigns knowledge on the matter.

"So, what's your plan for the future?" Don cuts right to the quick.

"I only talk business during banker's hours, Don," he says, drawing his name out in a mocking tone.

Everyone falls silent.

"Well, you and Grace haven't had a vacation in years. Don and I have been talking about a jaunt to the Cayman Islands. Wouldn't that be fun?" Lexi swoons.

"There's no time for relaxing. This lucky bastard is on a roll!" Don says, pointing at Robert.

Grace excuses herself.

"I'll come with you," Lexi says, following her.

"Hey Robert, you want some Saki?" Don flags down one of the cute Asian waitresses.

"Saki? They got whiskey in here?"

The waitress nods.

"Yeah, you know what? Make that two shots."

"Make it four," Robert sneers.

Don grabs the menu and peruses it quickly, retaining nothing. "Dinner for four. Make it up. Four of everything on the menu."

The waitress nods politely and leaves.

"She reminds me of a hooker masseuse that used to give me happy endings back in the day," Robert says as he watches the waitress walk away.

"That's funny I was thinking the same thing," Don says and the men share a laugh.

The women are cracking up in the bathroom.

"You're not serious!" Lexi gasps between laughter.

"I'm telling you! Four!" Grace wipes her eyes.

"I haven't had four orgasms all year. Well, not counting my own hand!"

When Grace's laughter abates, she says, "Oh, honey, I'm so sorry. Maybe if Robert had a word with him." They begin hysterical laughing all over again.

"Oh, stop. Don't tease just because your husband's making more money than mine."

Grace gets serious. "Lexi, you know I don't care about the money."

Lexi scoffs at Grace's sincerity and fixes her heavy makeup in the mirror. "Who doesn't love money?"

The men are engaged in conversation when the women return to the table. "So, Robert, you gotta hear this shit. It's so ironic. There's litigation against L-corp. Do you know what L-corp is?"

"Yeah, sure. Tell me."

"Some copyright infringement against Amnesty International. Right? And we're in court, Amnesty's rep is on the stand. Now, you gotta understand, Amnesty is this love the whales, save the world, non-profit organization. The rep failed to leave his Rolex at home. Who's going to notice with the best lawyers in Manhattan. The president of L-corp, in the middle of the rep's defense, starts projectile vomiting, all over the

38

desk. The rep doesn't even notice. Now, let's say the poor mother fucker was sick to his stomach, because he actually cares about doing the right thing, while his surrounding partners don't give a shit who they were hurting. But the rep keeps going, and what do you think the judge does?

"I don't know. What does he do?"

"He favors Amnesty. They're just another fuck fest. But I still got paid." They drink. "So how's the market, got any tips?"

"You want a tip? When you're up to your neck in shit, there's nothing to do but sing."

Lexi and Grace are ordering sake shots. "I had the idea before I was even pregnant with Franny. She is going to need ballet lessons, I said to myself. So, I took the money I was making at the time and invested it in a start up company that brings in fifteen k a month. Now, Francesca and Lucas can have everything I didn't have as a kid."

"You're a lucky woman." Grace lowers her head.

"I'm sorry, Grace. Is this upsetting you? I didn't mean to..."

"No, it's fine. I have my kids at school. I wouldn't trade them for anything."

Don persists. "I got these Knicks tickets on the floor, any time you need them, two and four seats."

"Cut the bullshit. Spell it out so we can move on."

Don leans in and lowers his voice, "I've been in this business a long time. Two days in a row like that is not a coincidence. I want in."

"Here's the deal. I'm going to run this office for a while. What I need from you is the best. Give me Brill's star list. Find me the one good guy that the rest of those morons have. I want to know who they're talking to. Then I'll take care of you."

"What are you two plotting?" Lexi interrupts.

"Me and Barry here were discussing –"

"Why are you calling him Barry? His name's Don," Lexi slurs, the sake kicking in.

"What's the difference?"

Grace gives Robert a look. Lexi continues, "Raymond thinks he knows everything. Gay as a jaybird. He's forgetting he hired me to design the place. I'm tired of fighting him on color composition and fabric swatches, so I let him go off. Oh, and he's good. For the first time, I allow my name to go where my work wasn't. I felt bad taking his money. I'm thinking now of offering him a job."

"How sweet."

"And he's so cute! I swear, why are gay man so sexy to me?"

"The unattainable urge to want what we can't have. It's not uncommon for women to want men who are unavailable. Our competitive nature wants to win."

The food arrives. Robert grabs several pieces of sashimi with his fingers and shoves them in his mouth rapidly. He smiles a big, toothy grin and says, "Hmmm. What does that taste like?"

Lexi gasps, "That's disgusting!"

"The chopsticks, Robert. They're there for a reason," Grace says in a tone reserved for her students.

"I've suddenly lost my appetite," Lexi says, exhaling gruffly.

"Lexi, if you want to criticize my husband, please speak to me privately."

"Excuse me, honey," Lexi tosses her napkin on the table.

"Whoa, she's got some set of balls on her, eh Robert?" Don chuckles.

Grace measures her words. "Don't confuse balls with pussy, Don. I am a woman, and I have a pussy. Pussy has all the power."

Robert continues chewing. He is looking into Grace's eyes. "That's what it tastes like," he says, cracking up while shoveling more food into his face.

Grace stares at Robert incredulously, silent.

Grace and Robert are walking to their car in silence. Robert opens the door for her. She gets in without a word. Robert joins her inside, returning her quiet stare. He goes to start the engine and stops. They continue looking deeply at each other. "Who are you and what did you do with my husband?" she asks softly. He leans in and softly kisses her neck. She reaches down and unfastening his pants. He grabs her by the hips and hoists her up on top of him. She slides her underwear to the side. They fumble for a moment. He enters her. They do not move.

"Oh my..." Robert exhales as Grace cries out from the pit of her guts. They reach an orgasm together. They stay in that position, holding each other.

Robert drives them home with Grace sitting against the passenger door, facing him. She is breathing heavy, doing her best to compose herself. She laughs out loud. Robert glances back and forth from her to the road. A chuckle escapes him. That makes her laugh harder. He continues to laugh with her.

"Robert, where did that come from? My God! I saw pyramids!"

"I gotta say, kid. I've never felt anything like that before," he says, as they drive home enjoying the silence between them.

VI

It's late in the day and the bell is about to ring. Robert sits at his desk with his feet up, exuding the confidence of a man who would enjoy watching the whole world burn. Placing the phone on the receiver, he spots Brill's right-hand man Jimmy pass by, looking frustrated. "Jimmy!" he pokes.

"Yeah?" Jimmy's expression is that of a scolded puppy. He doesn't want to stop but he knows it will only get worse for him if he doesn't.

Robert muses, "Having a tough time over there?"

"Uh... No."

"That new fiancé is not going to get the size ring she wants, huh? And she's not going to like that."

Jimmy is silent.

"How about a tip that makes you twenty grand. But only if you jerk off in that plant at the end of the day."

"What'd you say?"

"Twenty grand. To jerk off in that plant."

The other brokers overhear and start to gather around the desk. One broker says, "Hey, I'll do it. I'll jerk off in your mouth for ten grand." The surrounding brokers laugh.

Robert gets up and whispers something in Jimmy's ear. Sal walks over and tries to get close enough to listen. Robert stops and looks at him with disdain. "Sal, your breath smells like shit! Really, it's smells like ass. Hey, who shit in Sal's mouth?"

"Fuck you, dick," Sal says as he moves away, mumbling something under his breath.

"What was that? You want me to suck your dick? No wonder your breath smells like a shit. You've been eating ass all day, you dirty Guinea."

Sal comes at him with a fist. Robert effortlessly deflects the punch, smacking Sal twice across the face with an open hand. Robert gets in his face, nose to nose, and foams at the mouth. "You fucking pussy. Don't you ever come at me again," Robert says and turns his back on Sal, continuing to whisper in a terrified Jimmy's ear.

Sal backs away and returns to his desk, fuming.

Jimmy hurriedly returns to his desk and gets on the phone, quickly punching numbers into his computer.

Brokers continue making calls. The bell rings. Jimmy has made the twenty grand. Brokers congratulate Jimmy and throw glances at Robert, who stands, looking toward Mr. Harrison's office. Mr. Harrison is packing up to leave. He waves good-bye and gives proper congratulations to the brokers, giving special mention to Robert. He leaves.

"Oh boy," Robert says and lights a cigarette, staring at Jimmy.

"What. You weren't serious," Jimmy's voice shakes as he looks around for help. He finds none.

"Oh? Get over there now. That plant is looking mighty lonely." Robert is cool, motionless. Jimmy tries to stare him down. Robert doesn't move. "Or don't. There are a lot of guys in this office who will do it for you. You just have to give them the twenty grand. You know what, Jimmy? Don't do it."

43

Jimmy walks over to the plant. They all crowd around and egg him on.

Robert takes a front row position. "Oh, fun!" he says slapping his hands together.

Jimmy looks at Robert with uncertainty. He starts to unzip his fly. He takes his penis out and starts to squeeze it.

"What's wrong? Hey, has anyone got any Viagra?"

The other brokers laugh. Jimmy tries harder. A broker comes over with a Playboy magazine. He holds it up in front of Jimmy's face. The laughter continues.

"There you go. That's a little help. Come on, Jimmy. That's a naked woman. Jimmy... Jimmy? What's going on there? You're a faggot! Hey fellas, Jimmy likes it in the ass!" Robert roars.

A broker brings over another magazine and opens to a page with an advertisement of a male model wearing underwear. "Forget about the ring. Maybe you should be saving up your money for an apartment in the West Village!" They all burst out laughing.

Robert looks around. "Where are those strippers?"

Someone answers, "On the way up!"

Two skanky strippers wearing skimpy outfits step out off the elevator and Robert walks over to greet them. "Ladies! You're just in time!" They wrap their feather boas around his neck as he escorts them over to Jimmy, who is visibly showing signs of sweating in response to the continual jeering. "Hey girls, this man with his dick in his hand? If he doesn't jerk off in this plant, he's fired. He needs your help more than anyone's needed your help before. Right, Jimmy?"

"Yeah," his response is sullen.

"Okay, so how much, Jimmy? How much do you want to pay these girls to help you jerk off in this plant?"

"I don't know. Five hundred?"

The girls easily say yes. Robert stops them with a hand. "Girls! You give it away too easily! Don't be so fucking easy! That's what got you here in the first place!" Robert shakes his head.

"So how much should we ask for, since you're our manager now?" one of the strippers says, cackling.

"Well, I thought going into this, you girls were worth at least two grand apiece."

"Oh, Come on!" Jimmy contests.

The first stripper turns to the second and whispers, "Can we get that?"

Robert hears. "That and more. Don't underestimate your value! Jimmy, gimme five grand."

"Robert, I don't carry that kind of cash."

"That's ok because I do. But now you owe me." Robert takes out the cash and places it on a desk next to lines of coke the brokers are hovering over. The girls play out a sensual lesbian act. Jimmy watches them intently until he finally releases himself onto the heavily marbled leaves of the lush Chinese Evergreen. The men cheer. Jimmy falls to his knees, broken. Robert bends down and whispers in Jimmy's ear, "Hey buddy! I was just fucking with ya! You didn't have to do that. But you did. Now, it will stay with you forever. How does forever sound?"

Grace opens her office door to greet Mrs. Gordon, a black, exigently obese woman in her forties. She wears an ill-kept dress and ergonomic house slippers.

"Mrs. Gordon, it's nice to see you. Please come in," Grace smiles and steps aside to make room for Mrs. Gordon to enter, her large body moving painfully slow with the assistance of a walking cane. Grace waits patiently for her to sit before taking her seat. "Your daughter is such a unique girl. I believe she's one of our brightest students," Grace waits for Mrs. Gordon to respond, and when she doesn't, she continues, "but she is exhibiting behavioral issues, trouble listening, and that creates problems for our other students."

"I don't care nothin' 'bout no other students. I came all dis way to talk 'bout Aisha, din't I?" Mrs. Gordon breathes heavily.

"Absolutely, and I'm very glad you did. I wanted to talk to you about helping your daughter reach her potential. I think she needs an evaluation and maybe after a comprehensive assessment we can find the right medication that will help her concentrate better, if need be."

"Who's gonna pay for dat? I ain't got money for dat sounds expensive."

"I can help you make an appointment with Dr. Bob Perkins. He's had a front seat to the latest educational approaches for children struggling with executive function skill deficits and learning differences of all kinds. He works part time out of a free clinic in the area for those who can't afford treatment but are in need. I've worked with him before and he's a godsend."

"An whut makes you so shore Aisha need treatment? Sound like you the one could use some help. Maybe if yous betta at yo job instead of worryin' 'bout my Aisha, I be home watchin' One Life To Live."

"Mrs. Gordon, please understand. Discipline teaches children to follow rules and it starts in the

46

home. Your responsibility as a parent is to help your child become self-reliant, respectful, and self-controlled. Schools and health care professionals can help. But the primary responsibility for discipline rests with parents."

"You know whut the problem is with you white women is? You don know how ta deal with black chilren. They different from the white chilren."

Grace picks up the phone and dials. "Mrs. Thompson, could you please come to my office? I have Aisha's mother here. Thank you," she hangs up the phone. "Mrs. Thompson is Aisha's guidance counselor. I'd like for us to discuss with you some possibilities for your daughter."

"What you goin' tell me whas good for my daughta for. Don't bring anotha white woman in here, tell me what's good for Aisha," Mrs. Gordon fumes.

Mrs. Thompson enters the room. She is a strong black woman in her fifties in a power suit. She takes a moment to give Mrs. Gordon a once over. Mrs. Gordon whips her head away in mock frustration, mumbling to herself unintelligibly.

"Mrs. Gordon, this is Mrs. Thompson," Grace says with the sweep of her hand.

"Nice to meet you," Mrs. Thompson says stiffly.

"Mrs. Thompson, could you please explain the disciplinary problems we've been having with Aisha?"

"Sure, Mrs. Rice. Mrs. Gordon, your daughter is extremely hyperactive, she has problems concentrating in class and has atrocious manners. I recommend she be evaluated for attention deficit hyperactivity disorder and considered for medication."

"What I gotta do? Why cain't you do it? Ain't dat yo job? I don know nothin' 'bout teachin'. This ain't my fault. Dats yo job."

Grace interjects, "Our concern is for Aisha. There's no blame here. If you need help with your daughter, I am more than happy to help you. That's why we're here. We both want what's best for her." Grace writes down a phone number. "But I can't help your child without you. Think of it as if Aisha had a headache, you'd give her aspirin, right? Or for diabetes, people take insulin. If medicine will help cure her instability, we need to find that out. But I need you to commit some of your time. I can set up the appointment with Dr. Perkins right now. Are you willing to do this?"

"I'm fine wid it. An um, I was wunnering if I can have one of them candies you got?" Mrs. Gordon points to the bowl of hard candy on Grace's desk.

"Of course. Please help yourself."

Mrs. Gordon uses her swollen fingers to pluck four pieces of candy from the dish, piling all four of them into her mouth. Grace and Mrs. Thompson watch as she sucks noisily on them as a nursing baby would.

Grace arrives home, checks the mail, and listens to voice messages, a missed call from Lexi Osmond in particular. "Grace! We need a girl's night out! The men shouldn't have all the fun!" Grace dials her number.

Moments later, a knock at the front door summons Grace from upstairs, having changed into something softer. On the other side of the door, a smiley Lexi cradles two bottles of wine in one arm. "I didn't think one would be enough to get the job done," she says, hugging Grace with her free arm.

"That was fast! I didn't even have time to straighten up. I'm so embarrassed," she says, trying to clean an already spotless house.

"Oh, please! Get some glasses, pronto! The babysitter threatened mutiny if I stay out too late."

Grace grabs the glasses and the two women sit together on the white couch, feet up. Grace sighs. Lexi prods her with her foot. "So things seem to be looking up for you and Robert. I've never seen him so...feral."

"I had a talking to with him the other night. I was riding him harder than usual and something clicked. He is completely incensed with work now."

"That's great, Grace. But there's something more than that. I can't quite put my finger on it. I almost don't recognize him."

"Oh, he's my husband, alright. The man I always wanted him to be!"

Robert sits in front of fifteen shots of Jack Daniels at O'Henry's. He pounds them down, one after the other, to the chanting of brokers behind him. They hold bills in their hands, exchanging bets for how many shots he can get down. He finishes the row and the crowd erupts. He grabs a handful of money, grabs two girls and sticks one stack in one girl's cleavage, the other stack down the other girl's pants, pulls them close, and starts making out with the both of them.

"Can you imagine your husband actually listening?"

"Here here!" Lexi holds up her wine glass to toast, "I still can't get Don to put the toilet seat down!"

Robert sits at the end of the bar with a fresh drink. The other brokers have gone except Sal, who sits to his right. "With your trading skills, my public relations and organizational abilities, we can open our own office. We'll do the hiring, we'll do the firing, we'll keep the profits, fifty-fifty. You know what kind of money we're talking?"

Robert stares straight ahead, bleary-eyed and unresponsive.

Sal continues, "Look, I'll set everything up. I'll do all the legwork, the computer systems. I'll find the space and get the best young guys in the city under us. All you gotta do is just step into the office and trade. That's it. And of course, help me bankroll it.

"Hey Sal, go fuck yourself." Robert polishes off his drink and staggers out.

Grace and Lexi are polishing off the second bottle of wine when they hear the sound of Robert's car driving onto the front lawn and crashing into the side of Grace's car parked in the driveway with a screeching of brakes. They jump to their feet and run out the front door. Robert stumbles out of the car.

"Robert!" Grace screams.

"Oh hello, wife. And friend of wife. I love this life. Now, this is a good life. Much better than that other one. And you," Robert crawls over to Grace. "This body has no tolerance for liquor!" Robert rolls over on his back and starts singing, "Oh Danny boy the pipes the pipes are calling!" They inspect the damaged cars.

"Ooh. That hurts," Lexi whistles.

"Oh yeah, baby," Robert tries to stand and face plants on the lawn.

"I see you have things all under control," Lexi laughs mockingly.

Lights come on in adjacent homes. A neighbor calls out, "Is everything okay over there?"

A second neighbor chimes in, "Is anyone hurt?"

50

"Everything's fine, thanks," Grace answers, embarrassed.

"Does he need a doctor? Should we call an ambulance?"

"No, no. He's just had too much to drink."

"What is he, drunk? He shouldn't be driving if he's been drinking."

"Thank you. I'm well aware. Come on, Robert. Get up," Grace pleads.

Lexi grabs her arm. "I see a nice, new car on the horizon."

Robert rolls over on his back and continues singing.

"I've got to put my rock star husband to bed."

"But you do see what I mean about him, right? He's...different."

"He's blowing off some steam. But I tell you. Just because he's making some money now, I won't let him ruin our lives over stupidity. Good night."

"Good night, dear. And good luck!" Lexi hugs her and heads home.

Grace sighs, helping Robert into the house and up to bed. He is laughing and singing sadistically. She manages to get him onto the bed just as he passes out. She begins to undress him. A huge smile is spread across his face. She strokes his hair tenderly and kisses him gently. "My messy husband. What am I going to do with you?"

The next morning, Grace is in the kitchen nursing a hangover with a cup of coffee. She begins straightening up the house from the night before, collecting the wine glasses from the living room and gathering clothes from the bedroom floor, throwing them into a laundry basket. She checks the pockets before dumping them in the machine and comes across Robert's shirt from the night before, lipstick smeared all over the shirt's collar.

"Damn it!" she cries, storming out.

Robert lays naked, spread eagle across the mattress. Grace leaps on the bed and grabs Robert by his balls, thrusting his shirt in his face. Robert's eyes pop open, bulging out of his head. "What the fuck? Is this a fucking cliché? Are you fucking kidding me?" Grace is twisting his scrotum, her knuckles whitening. Robert is breathless, trying to utter a retort. There is the sound of scuttling bugs fills the room. "If you're cheating on me, your life is not worth shit. I will not have it, you son of a bitch!"

Beads of blood start to build on Robert's forehead. Robert cannot speak. His eyes roll back in his head and blood begins to stream down his face. His face contorts. "Grace, help me," the small voice he produces echoes from far away.

"Robert?" she whispers, letting go of her grip. She stands back, wiping the tears from her face, stunned. Robert sits up, wipes the blood off his brow, and runs to the bathroom. Splashing water on his face, he stares at himself in the mirror. Under the spots of blood, there is nothing. His forehead is smooth and unmarked.

Grace is banging on the door. "Robert, are you okay? Answer me! I'm calling 911!"

"Don't call 911. I'm okay. Give me a minute. I'll be fine. Relax." Robert takes a moment to compose himself in the mirror.

The scuttling insect sound is gone. Grace is weeping. Robert opens the door and she runs to him, hugging him tightly. His arms remain open, held out at his sides. "I'm so sorry! Did I hurt you? Are you okay?

If anything happened to you, I don't know what I'd do. Please, talk to me."

"It's alright, I just hit my head in the car accident last night, and uh, you must have aggravated it."

"Are you sure? We should go to the hospital."

"Forget about it. I'm fine, everything's fine."

Grace pulls him tighter, and whimpers on his shoulder. He regards this for a moment. He looks down at her, smells her hair, and slowly wraps his arms around her and holds her. He buries his face in her hair. "Robert, I want an explanation. Why is there lipstick stains on your shirt?" she says through tears.

"That was a girl from work. She was just playing around. We were celebrating. It was nothing. Go downstairs and call us a cab."

"Where are we going?"

"I have a surprise for you."

"What kind of surprise?"

"The kind that fixes problems. Call in sick, take the day off. This will be our day."

"I can't! I have things to take care of!"

"I guess you don't need a new car then."

"Robert!" Grace hugs him and runs out excited. Robert goes to the closet and grabs a briefcase. He pushes the bed out the way, opens the makeshift safe, and moves aside a handgun on top of the pile of money. He begins loading money into the briefcase.

Grace is in the kitchen, rapidly talking into the phone, "Hello, Lois? Reschedule all my appointments. I'm not feeling well."

"Most of them can be rescheduled, but you know how Mrs. Gordon is," Lois smirks.

"That's today? Shit. Oh, I'm sorry, Lois. I didn't mean to swear. Just call and uh… Look, just reschedule it for next week."

Grace and Robert are snuggled up in the backseat of a taxi. They pull into a Mercedes dealership. Grace starts to jump up and down in her seat with excitement.

The salesman is smiling ear to ear at Robert as Grace runs through the showroom. She finds the one she wants and climbs in.

"Looking for a new car for the Mrs.? She has good taste," the salesman chides.

"You think?"

"Oh yeah, this Mercedes SL 600 Roadster is built on its own platform, a first for this Mercedes. The new SL boasts standard lock brakes with electrohydraulic actuation. A first for any car."

"You don't say."

"Yessir. It has an onboard computer that adjusts brake pressure to each wheel as needed for optimal stops in all conditions."

Grace calls from across the showroom, "Robert, I love it. I want this one!"

"Of course, Darling. Whatever you want."

"Shall I write it up?"

Robert's cell phone rings. "I'm not finished with you yet. Hold on," he says to the salesman. He answers the phone. "Yeah?"

"Hey, it's me, Sal."

"Hello, Sal. Do you want my dick in your ass? Is that really why you keep bothering me? I knew you were gay the moment I met you."

"What the fuck is wrong with you?"

"Don't you worry 'bout me. Let's make money," he says, hangs up the phone, and turns back to the stunned salesman. "Continue."

"What do you mean, continue? The lady wants the car, no?" the salesman stammers.

"What do you think, I'm going to pay eighty-thousand in cash..."

"Fully loaded, one twenty-three."

"I'm not going to pay that kind of money without some convincing. I know Mercedes is the best. Where's your manager?"

The salesman looks at him, sheepishly. "Sir, I'm certain I can take care of this for you."

"No, you're fired. Get me the manager."

The salesman walks away in a huff. Robert looks around with a grin. The salesman comes back with a manager. "What can I do for you today, Mr...?"

"Rice. You're selling a car for six figures in this dump and this putz is reading the Consumer's Report as a sales pitch."

The manager takes Robert to the side. "Mr. Rice, I see where you're coming from. You want to get the Mrs. off your back, shut her up for a while? Mercedes is the perfect sedative for any domestic feud. The seats fully recline, and with the leather interior, it's an easy cleanup."

"Now that's the way to sell a car. Do you have black on black?"

"Of course," the manager replies.

"Do you take cash?" Robert lifts up the briefcase.

"Name one business in America that doesn't."

"I'll take two. And whatever the wife wants. And I want them ready to drive out of here."

"Right away," the manager says, motioning the salesman to start the paperwork.

Grace's drives her new silver convertible, top down, at a comfortable pace. She is appreciating the look and feel of the exquisite machine. Robert drives at a close distance behind her. He catches up and turns to her, calling out, "Let's see what you can do with the power, Grace!" He rockets down the street, music blaring. From out of nowhere, like a cannonball, Grace passes him as if he were standing still. Robert smiles.

Robert and Grace enter through the front door of their home carrying packages. They are laughing. Robert sticks his hand down the back of her pants. She yelps, "What are you doing?"

"I want that ass!"

"Should I open a bottle of wine?"

"Wine? Whiskey!"

"Okay, slow poke." She laughs, and fixes them a drink.

"You wanna go again?"

"Oh, stop it. Don't be a sore loser."

Robert sits comfortably on the couch as Grace brings over his drink. She lights candles, preparing the mood for them. He watches the way she moves, enticed by her beauty. She sits next to him, smiling softly. The top of her blouse has unbuttoned and her breasts are showing. Robert gives her a look.

"Yes? What's that look?"

"I don't know what it is. I love the way you move."

Grace blushes. She gives him a soft kiss on the lips. She pulls away. He follows. He wants more. "Wait, I want to tell you a story. Remember Aisha? The girl from my school?"

Robert grabs her forcefully and pulls her to him. She resists and he grabs her by the hair, pulling her down.

"Robert! What's the matter with you? You're hurting me!"

"C'mon. Let's fuck."

"Robert, what is this? What are you, possessed?"

"Funny you should mention that."

"What's that supposed to mean?"

"I'm not possessed. But Robert is."

"Cute. Okay. To whom am I speaking with?"

"I'd prefer it if you called me Nash. That's my real name. I never liked the name Robert."

"I wonder how your father would feel about that."

"My father's name was Burt. He was a real prick."

"Your father is still alive and his name is Robert, same as yours. And this game you're playing is starting to annoy me. If this is your new way of trying to turn me on, it's not working." She tries to stand, but he grabs her hand, pulling her back down.

"Let me ask you a question. Do you like that car?"

"Yes. I love my car. Thank you."

"Don't you want more?"

"What do you mean?"

"You want it all, don't you?"

"Who doesn't want it all?"

"Good. That's the first step to us having everything we want. Admitting that we want it."

"Where do you want to start?"

"First thing, we should satisfy no one but ourselves."

"That's a little harsh, don't you think?"

"If you can't get past the first step, there's no way into it at all."

"I get satisfaction helping other people,"Grace says with conviction.

"The time you spend helping others, you lose time spent on yourself."

"But I am helping myself by helping them. Let me give you an example. Take Aisha. The girl suffers from borderline schizophrenia, I suspect. She has yet to be diagnosed. She comes from a poor, black family..."

"Why do you give a shit about those niggers?"

"Robert! I will not have you use that word in my house. Ever!"

"Fine, okay. How about this, you can't teach a monkey to act like a human. Get it through your head."

"How dare you! Where is this coming from? Who are you to say such vile things? You have an education, for Christ's sake! Where is your consideration for others less fortunate?"

"In my ass. What have those people ever done for anybody besides their own kind? They use the slave card every chance they get."

"This conversation is over." Grace stands and climbs the stairs, two at a time.

Robert calls after her, "Oh, c'mon. You know it's true. Why deny what I'm saying. You know what you want. Stop denying your primal feelings. Don't get upset. We've had such a great day today. I just got you a beautiful car."

"Stick the car where your consideration is!" she screams, locking the bedroom door behind her.

Robert sits on the couch and finishes his drink. He walks upstairs to the bedroom and tries to open the bedroom door. "Grace, open the door." There is no answer from inside the bedroom. Robert's temper rises. "Grace, open the fucking door!"

"Robert, there's a guest bedroom. I suggest you use it."

Robert starts banging on the bedroom door. "Open this door, dear. Open this fucking door! Right fucking now!" The banging continues.

"Robert, you're scaring me. Stop it! Go to sleep. We'll talk tomorrow."

Robert stops. He is breathing heavy. He paces the hallway, calming himself down. He opens the door to the guest room and throws himself onto the bed, tossing and turning. He gets up, goes downstairs, and grabs the bottle of Jack Daniels. He returns to the guest bedroom, takes off his clothes, and sits on the edge of the bed in his underwear. He lights a cigarette and takes several swigs from the bottle, deep in thought.

VII

Robert is sleeping listlessly. He hears the sound of a car pulling up to the front of the house. He jumps up and looks out the window in time to see Grace getting into a taxi in her work attire. "Ah, shit," he says.

David Brill walks through the room with his head down. "Hey Brill, I bet Sal you weren't a dead beat. And I lost," Brian Beckerman lobs. David continues walking, defeated.

Robert sits at the chair in his new office, staring into nothing. Brokers are poking their heads in with caution, looking for a moment to garner his attention. Sal confidently pops in for a visit.

"Hey, how's Mars? Are you still a scumbag, in that world you're in?"

Robert snaps to. "Scumbag, huh? I'm a scumbag? I bet I can get you to shine my shoes for a stock tip right now, you fucking loser."

"I'll do it for forty k."

Robert gets an idea. He looks at Sal. "Alright, Saaaal. For forty k, you gotta clean 'em with your tongue and polish 'em with your tie."

Sal looks at him, thinking for a moment. "Gimmee your shoes."

"Nah, get down on your knees and take 'em off."

"Son of a bitch," Sal says, roughly taking off his tie. He painfully gets down on his knees and begins licking Robert's shoes, making an ugly face. Robert is looking down on him, half-grinning.

Robert moves around the office, untouchable. Stopping at the desk of a Mark Rosenshwag, a stereotypical Jewish broker on the verge of a breakdown, he says, "Rosenshwag! Boy, someone must've really hated your kind for giving you that awful name!"

"Watch yourself, Rice. I've seen 'em up, I've seen 'em down. You're up now. Doesn't mean the tides can't turn."

"Ah, I like your moxie."

"What do you want, Robert? I'm busy."

"You wanna make fifty grand?"

"I'm not going to play your games. I've got a little pride left."

"How about sixty grand? You're down thirty on the day already. Sixty will send you home happy."

Rosenshwag thinks on it. "Okay, what?"

60

"Piss yourself. Sit there and piss your fucking pants."

"Fuck you! Who do you think you are? I've been here for ten fucking years!"

"Oh, but Mark, I can feel that ulcer eating away at your stomach. I can feel the churn. Why not let it up a little. You want some relief, don't you? A release from the pressure?"

"Ninety. I'll do it for Ninety thousand."

"Seventy-five."

"Eighty-five."

"Done."

Rosenshwag looks up at Robert. He picks up a bottle of water and finishes the entire thing. Other brokers take notice and encourage the deal. Rosenshwag sits, legs shaking. He closes his eyes tightly, shaking his legs, pushing. Robert stops him.

"Enough. Go to the head before you piss yourself."

"What about the tip?"

"You're a veteran. Do the work. Don't embarrass yourself." Robert returns to his office to grab his jacket. Brokers run after him, screaming to Robert for tips. They follow him into the elevator, clamoring after him.

"How much if I shit myself?"

"I'll eat my shit for a grand!"

Robert shoves them out of the elevator with sub-human physical strength. They are tossed to the side, only to allow more room for other brokers to approach him before the doors to the elevator close in their face to a disgusted Robert.

Grace has a bullhorn, controlling the kids on the school playground at recess. Little girls hold onto

Grace's legs with happiness and delight. She is loved and it shows.

Robert pulls up in his new Mercedes just outside of school property. Grace has turned her head to see a fight starting on the far edge of the playground between Aisha and a group of boys, teasing and hitting her. Before she can reach it, Robert enters the playground and stops the fight. He consoles a crying Aisha, appearing to give her some valuable advice. Robert looks up and locks eyes with Grace, waving, and wipes Aisha's tears away.

Close up, Aisha is eyeballing Robert. "What's your real name?"

"Nash."

"How long have you been up here?" Aisha studies him. She looks around to see if anyone is watching, sees the principal and smiles. "It's so much better than down there, isn't it?"

Robert stares at her, silent.

"I couldn't figure out why I was put in a sweet, little innocent girl's body. For a long time I thought it was a mistake. I mean, I live a life of poverty and my mother is lump of shit with feet. I have to deal with kids all day. What the hell do you talk about with eight year olds? I didn't know what I was supposed to be doin'."

"So, did you figure it out?"

"Oh yeah! This is great! I can get away with everything, and no one can do anything about it. 'Cause I'm a kid!"

"I've been thinking that there's more to it."

"Whateva'. All I know is I'm enjoying myself. Isn't that what he told us to do?"

"Yeah, but to what end?"

"Don't think it's forever. 'Cause it ain't."

62

Grace approaches. "What are you two talking about?"

Aisha walks off with a look at Robert over her shoulder. "See ya around, Nash."

"Oh, so it's Nash now. No wonder why you two get along. You're both nuts. You do realize that was Aisha you were talking to. How selfless of you."

Miss Lewis makes her way over to where Grace and Robert are talking. "Mrs. Rice, should I get the kids in line?"

"No, thank you. I've got them, Miss Lewis."

"You must be Grace's husband."

"Nash."

"Hello, Nash. I'm Miss Lewis. I've heard so much about you."

Grace snaps, "His name is Robert."

"Nash, your name is Robert?"

"His name is not Nash. Stop doing that! Stop telling everyone your name is Nash!"

"He wants to be Nash, let him be Nash. I personally like the name."

"How nice for you. Could you give my husband and I a moment please?"

Miss Lewis walks off, with a lingering look at Robert. Robert stares after her and Grace notices the hold. Irritated, she asks, "What do I owe the pleasure?"

"I thought maybe you needed a ride home."

"Maybe Miss Lewis would like a ride."

"She's got a nice ass, but it ain't yours." Robert pulls her to him and kisses her. The surrounding kids start to howl and giggle. Grace pulls away quickly.

"Not in front of the kids," she blushes, turning to usher the children inside using the bullhorn. "Alright. Line up. Let's go!"

Robert lounges at Grace's desk, feet up. Grace busies herself around him, gathering things for a meeting. "Robert, I have to handle some business. Are you alright here? Do you need anything?"

Robert reaches for a cigarette.

"Don't even think about it," Grace slaps his feet off her desk. "I'll be back in an hour. Then we can go. There's a teacher's lounge on the second floor, room 208, if you get thirsty."

"I want to eat your ass."

She gives him an opened mouth gasp, "Oh, my!" She covers her open mouth in feigned bashfulness, playing at composing her chastity. She smirks at him and exits.

Robert looks around her desk, opening drawers. He finds a photo envelope buried under some papers. He shuffles through them. He stops on a picture of himself wearing a Hawaiian shirt and khaki shorts, a tropical location behind him. The expression in the photo is soft and easy going. The next photo he stops on is of Robert and Grace on the deck of a cruise, drinks in hands and big smiles on their faces. He focuses on Grace's smile. He picks up the phone and dials. "Sal, I need a favor... Don't worry, do me right, I'll do you right. I want to go to Vegas. Set it up for me, the best of the best. I want high roller status... Fuck you, you are my bitch. Get it done."

Robert wanders the school hallways, peering in on the classrooms. He finds the teacher's lounge and enters. Mr. Connor, a math teacher, grades papers. Robert walks over to the soda machine and grabs a coke. He sits directly across from Mr. Connor, staring at him. "How you doin'?"

Mr. Connor glances up and says, "Fine. You a sub?" he says and goes back to marking up papers, heavy on the red ink.

"Nah, I'm a rep from the Board Of Education. Happy here?"

Mr. Connor stops, putting his pen down. "Well, there are issues, but I'm sure you've heard it all."

"Humor me."

"Actually, we could use better access to the copier. It takes three days to get any copes made. I'm spending my tremendous teacher's salary at Kinko's. Does the Board give a shit?" Mr. Connor implores.

"Quit your bitchin'. Nobody made you take this job."

"Excuse me?"

Miss Lewis enters the room. She has a bag lunch.

"Why, hello there, Miss Lewis!" Robert beams.

"Enjoying your visit with us?"

"Yeah, it's so damn exciting, I'm barely containing myself."

Miss Lewis smiles and joins them at the table.

Robert continues, "Might I say, Miss Lewis, you redefine the hot for teacher fantasy. I'm sure a lot of little boys have had their first erections over you. You're one hellava teacher."

Mr. Connor lets a laugh escape him. He composes himself, gathering his papers. "Maybe I did choose the wrong profession. Maybe I should work for the Board of Ed," Mr. Connor says and exits quickly.

"I think he needs to get laid," Robert says.

"I think you're right. By the way, thanks for the compliment."

"You think that's a compliment? How 'bout this. You have a great ass. And a great set of tits. I can't tell which is nicer."

"Excuse me?"

"Excuse me? Excuse you. Stand up and turn around, I want to see what's better, your tits or that ass."

Miss Lewis thinks for a second. She stands and slowly turns around, keeping her eyes locked on his.

"So, which is better? Which do you like better?"

"I don't know. How old are you?"

"Why are you flirting with me?"

"Flirting? Was I flirting? I don't know what you mean. I thought we were just talking."

"Is that how you talk to women?"

"Do you like it?"

"Yes. But you're married to my boss."

"That I am. So what's your point?"

"Who are you?"

"Do you party?"

"Why?"

"Well, if you want, every day at 4 o'clock I go to O'Henry's for drinks. It's on 40 Wall Street, under my office," Robert takes out a piece of paper from his wallet, writes down the address, and hands it to her.

"What should I expect?"

"A bunch of girls and guys with a shit load of money having a lot fun."

"That sounds enticing."

"Now, if you will excuse me, I have an important date with the principal. Can't keep her waiting, if you know what I mean."

"Have a nice weekend, Nash."

Grace is seated at her desk. Robert walks in with a smile on his face. She returns his smile. "Did you get sent to the principal's office?'

"Yeah, I was bad boy."

"I guess I'll have to issue you a detention for the weekend."

"Oh that's too bad. I was planning a trip to Vegas."

"Las Vegas?

"I'll make you a deal. You get me out of detention, I'll take you with me."

Grace runs to Robert, jumping into his arms and overshoots the mark, propelling them backwards against the wall. They knock over a bookshelf and as they fall to the floor, books tumble on top of them. When their laughter and the falling books subside, Grace covers his face with silly girl kisses.

A limo pulls up to the Bellagio Hotel and Grace and Robert emerge, the bellhop quick to greet them and gather their bags. Grace walks ahead, as Robert addresses the overweight, black mustachioed limo driver. "Get me an eight ball," he says while handing him wad of cash. He catches up to Grace.

The penthouse room has a panoramic view overlooking the Vegas strip. Grace and Robert walk in. She is thrilled, but hesitates. "Oh my God. We can't afford this!"

"Grace, do you know how much money I made this week?"

"How could I possibly know? You don't tell me."

"First step in making money is spending money."

"I'll buy that." Grace disappears into the bathroom.

Robert gets on the phone. "Great. Good. Thanks." He calls out to Grace. "What size dress are you?"

She responds from the bathroom, "I'm still a four, Robert."

The room is filled with carts of food. Six dresses wrapped in plastic hang from the mirror. Boxes of shoes and pieces of jewelry are strewn about. A bottle of champagne has been opened and Robert and Grace sit comfortably on the bed together. "Oh, to live like this forever," Grace sighs.

"We can. We just have to play by the rules."

"I'm listening."

"If somebody tries to take away your joy, you stick it in their ass."

"Lovely."

"Believe half of what you see, none of what you hear."

"A little paranoid, but I'll entertain that."

"It's a good life, if you don't weaken and worry about repercussions."

The doorbell rings. Robert answers the door to a now sweaty limo driver. He hands Robert an envelope and Robert forks over some more cash. "This is for you." The driver takes the cash with a wave of his hand and Robert closes the door. He rips open the envelope onto a glass tabletop in the middle of the room and a pile of white powder wafts out.

"Oh, Jesus, Robert, come on. What is that? I don't want you to."

"We're on vacation, land of indulgence. Are you in, or are you out? Tell me my girl can't play a little. You deserve to live it up. Let's have some fun."

She lets out a deep breath, "I've never done it before."

"That's why you should try it, goose."

Her face breaks into a smile, despite herself. "Maybe just this once. When in Vegas, right?" she says, her voice shaking a bit. She follows his lead by bending over and taking some cocaine into her nose through a rolled up hundred-dollar bill. Her widened eyes reflect her stunned reaction as the drug hits her system. Robert scoops her up, and throws her onto the bed, kissing her exposed skin. She closes her eyes and feels deeply everything around her and loves the unencumbered invincibility. For the first time, she feels like the self she's always known herself to be.

The concierge escorts a tightly arm-locked Robert and Grace through the casino. Grace is breathtaking, working the dress and turning heads. Robert is wearing the most expensive suit he could find. They hold their heads high, grinning ear to ear. The concierge leads them to a private VIP room. They enter and the door is shut behind them, security standing guard.

The room is full of eccentrics and elites, sitting at tables, speaking in hushed tones. The concierge walks them over to the roulette table. Grace looks on nervously as Robert places huge bets, winning every time. As the pile grows, she fidgets, not sure what to do with her hands. A scantily clad cocktail waitress refreshes the Jack Daniels on the rocks for Robert, a white wine for Grace. She grabs it with both hands, gulping it. He flirts with the waitress, making the waitress blush. He tips her generously, tapping his cheek with a forefinger. She leans in to kiss him on the cheek upon his request, just a peck, but he grabs her chin, turning his face and kissing her wetly on the mouth. Grace lowers her glass and, seeing the kiss, throws what's left of her wine in their faces, and storms out. Robert collects his chips with a smile and a shrug and follows her out.

Grace storms through the casino to an elevator, Robert at her heels. They board the next car and stare straight ahead in silence. Grace is holding back tears. Robert peers at her from the corner of his eye. "So, I shouldn't do that?" he asks meekly.

Instead of blowing up at him, she laughs. He smiles and takes her hand in his, kissing it. She shakes her head. "No, you shouldn't kiss other women, you idiot." With his other hand he takes out a folded up piece of paper. He opens it and taps some coke on her down turned hand. She attempts to snort it, but misses, "Ok, I can't find my own nose," she says, laughing.

Robert dips his fingers into the powder and pinches it twice, one for each nostril, and replaces it inside the pocket of his suit jacket. He sniffs loudly to clear his passages, clapping his hands together as the elevator door opens up to the entrance the hotel nightclub. Robert heads straight for the doorman and tips him handsomely. They are immediately ushered in past the waiting partygoers.

The main room is packed with people dancing and drinking to excess. Grace and Robert walk onto the dance floor and slowly begin to move their bodies to the sexy house music. Others see them and make room for the hot couple. Their eyes are locked, visibly captivated with each other, their faces never far apart. They garner the attention of an older, seductive couple. Together, they dance with wild abandon.

They follow the couple to a plush hotel suite filled with half naked beautiful people dancing to even sexier music. The piles of food provided remain untouched as the attendees chase their high with drugs and booze.

70

Robert disappears into the crowd and Grace walks out onto the terrace, stretching her arms out over the glorious view. The man from the couple walks out onto the terrace and wraps his arms around Grace from behind her. She enjoys it, thinking it's Robert, but turns around and catches herself.

"Hi there," he whispers, gently.

"Hello."

"Your husband told me he wants to watch me fuck you." He dances close to her, pressing himself hard against her. She looks behind him for Robert and sees him with the wife from the couple. Robert's face is very close to the woman's and she seems to be enjoying the intimacy he provides. Grace waves her hands until Robert notices her. He walks outside and they all stand, staring at each other.

"I want you to repeat what you just said," Grace says to the man.

The man is silent, looking from Robert to Grace.

"Is it true? Did you say you wanted to watch him fuck me? I want to know," Grace manages. Robert is silent. "Come here, I want to talk to you." She pulls Robert by the hand to the far end of the terrace and sits him down, facing her. "Have you ever seen the film Contempt?" she asks. He shakes his head. "Brigitte Bardot, arguably one of the most beautiful woman in all of film. Married to a struggling writer. Enter big shot Hollywood Director Jack Palance who likes what he sees and asks the husband if he can take his wife for a ride in his fancy sports car. Husband says yeah, sure. He wants to get his movie made, right? Well, that's the end. It's not the end of the movie, but it's the end for them. Do you get it? Is that what you want?"

He is silent.

She sighs. "Let's get out of here."

Grace falls back in her lingerie, eyes closed, feeling the soft bed cover. Robert approaches the bed, stopping at the foot of it. He slowly starts to take his jacket off, watching Grace as she moves her body, her arms raised above her head and stretching. He slowly unbuttons his shirt, with a look of desire on his face. He throws the shirt to the floor, and kneels on the bed, moving towards her. He sits above her, placing a hand on her tit roughly. She doesn't react, but continues to move at her own pace, an internal rhythm. Robert sits above her, looking on. His face changes, softens, as he slowly puts his hands on her hips and lowers his head to her stomach. He rests it there. She opens her eyes and looks down at Robert. She looks upward, making a circle with both hands. She places the circle slowly above his head. She closes her eyes, and smiles.

Birds chirp over the quiet home of Grace and Robert Rice. Grace walks out of the front door with her briefcase and gets into her Mercedes. Robert calls to her from the upstairs window.

"Don't take any shit from those little punks."

"My little babies?"

"Give 'em hell, goose!"

"Crush the day, my love. I'll see you for dinner," she blows him a kiss and drives off.

Grace walks through the empty hallway to her office. Passing by the classroom of Miss Lewis, she hears her voice coming from inside. "I know you Wall Street types," Miss Lewis says with a giggle. Grace stops and peers in at Miss Lewis on her cell phone. Grace ducks out of view. Miss Lewis continues, "I'll try to sneak out early. Motorcycles are cool." Grace strains to hear more. There is silence. Grace gains her composure and continues walking.

Miss Lewis is teaching her 4th grade class. The students are relaxed and participating in the lesson. The room is filled with color. Pictures from the children hang on the walls. There are gerbils running in a wheel in a glass cage. The environment is comforting.

"Okay, did anyone get to the bonus question in last night's homework? There's a surprise in it for you if you can come up to the board and solve it." The children's hands go up, waving as they make excited sounds, wanting to be picked.

"Pick me!" says one student.

"Miss Lewis! Ooh Ooh!" says another.

Miss Lewis beams at her students. "Oh boy. I think I should make the bonus a little harder. You guys are too smart for me. Paul? Do you want to give this one a shot?"

"That's ok, Miss Lewis. You can give it to someone else."

"Paul, I know you can do it."

"Paul's retarded," Aisha interrupts. The class laughs.

"That's enough, Aisha. Come on, Paul. Show me what you got." He climbs off his chair and walks to the front of the room. Miss Lewis hands him a piece of chalk. He begins to solve the math problem with ease. Miss Lewis looks on with an assuring smile.

Grace walks in and takes a seat in the back of the room. Everyone stops what they're doing and the room falls quiet. Grace pulls out a notebook and a pen. "Please continue, everyone," she says, beginning to take notes.

Paul freezes, feeling the spot light.

"Let's show the principle how smart you are, Paul. You can do it."

"I forget."

"That's alright. Will someone else come up and finish the problem?" The children are quiet. No one raises a hand. "Anybody? Come on, you all had your hands up before. What happened to my class of geniuses?" Miss Lewis sighs. "Fine. We're going to play a game. I want you to close your eyes, all of you, and count to ten. When you open your eyes, it's just going to be you and me. The principle will be gone from the room. Don't look back. Just keep your eyes on me. Are you ready?" The children all close there eyes and start counting to ten, except Aisha. She is furiously scribbling at her desk. When they get to ten they open their eyes and smile. "Now, who's ready?"

The hands go up again with confidence.

"Great. That's more like it!"

Aisha turns around to Grace and gives her the finger. She mouths 'fuck you' and holds up the picture she was drawing. It depicts an evil faced Grace as the devil, in her business suit with horns and a tail. Grace responds immediately. She stands up and snatches the picture, violently grabbing the child by her arm and dragging her out of the classroom. Aisha hysterically laughs as Grace drags her down the hallway and into an empty room, locking the door. She folds the picture up and hides it in her jacket pocket.

Miss Lewis approaches Grace on the playground. "I never got a memo on any formal observation."

"That's the nature of an informal observation."

"Where is my student?"

"It's seems she didn't care for your meditation game."

"I love my class, Grace. They're doing so well this year, including Aisha. We got through the long division section in a week. I think that's a personal record."

"I'm sorry, do I look interested?"

"Where's Aisha?"

"I locked her in a detention room. She is uncontrollable."

"Unsupervised? Is that how we're handling our troubled students now? Locking them in rooms?"

"You're not telling me how to do my job, are you?"

Miss Lewis glares at Grace. Grace walks off, towards the direction of the school. She makes her way to the detention room and unlocks the door. Aisha sprints out at full speed, nearly knocking Grace over. "Goddammit!" Grace hollers, chasing after the girl down a flight of stairs, through various hallways.

"Burn in hell, muthafucka'!" Aisha yells out, followed by boisterous laughter.

Grace, winded, follows her into Miss Lewis' classroom. She stops at the door, searching the room. "Aisha?"

Aisha is seated at the teacher's desk, pulling papers out of drawers and writing red F's across the tops of them.

"If you disrupt my school again, I'm going to punch you in your fucking face."

"You can't talk to me like that. You's suppose to be the teacher."

"I can't teach an animal like you."

Aisha's head tilts to one side, eyes narrowed. When next she speaks, her voice adopts a deeper register, male, and wise beyond her eight years. "Well, now.

How very interesting. The pretty white woman trying to help all the poor black children and she can't even see five inches in front of your face. You think I'm bad? You don't even know what bad is! If you did, woman, you'd see you're living with it every damn day!"

"Pack your things. I'm calling your mother to pick you up. I don't ever want to see you in my school again!"

"I'm not going anywhere 'til I eat my lunch. Lookee here. Pinkies. My favorite," Aisha casually walks over to the gerbil cage. She reaches a hand in and pulls out a writhing, hairless baby gerbil. She eyes it closely before popping it in her mouth. She chews quickly, reaching for another one as Grace stares, shocked. Aisha talks with her mouth full. "Little piggies in a blanket, without the dough, yo. Could use some mustard, tho."

"Sweetheart, don't!"

"Sweetheart?" Aisha reaches into the cage and pulls out the mother gerbil. The squealing animal squirms in her hand as she raises it to her mouth and bites its head off. Blood pours out of the little severed body and stains Aisha's shirt as she chews the skull. "Please don't make me go. I have to leave all this? Boo hoo."

Grace turns and runs. She sprints to her office and orders her secretary, "Get Aisha's mother down here! Now!" Grace gets on the loudspeaker. "Security to room 202. Security to room 202."

"Is everything alright, Mrs. Rice?" the secretary says, startled.

Grace runs out, in the direction of Mrs. Thompson's office. She throws the door open, flustered. "Gail, I did not touch that girl!"

Miss Lewis has brought her class back from recess. They are standing in single file against the wall. Miss

Lewis opens the door and hears sobbing coming from inside, "Class, stay here and be quiet."

Miss Lewis is standing over a crying Aisha, huddled in the corner, helpless. A security guard arrives along with the school nurse, who kneels down beside her.

"What happened to you, dear?" the nurse inquires, concerned.

"Mrs. Rice... She hurt me real good."

Grace runs in and the adults turn to her.

"Grace, what happened to this child?"

"She was eating gerbils. That blood is not hers."

"There are puncture wounds all over her chest and face."

"What? That's impossible. She did that to herself!"

Aisha looks up and sees Grace. "She's gonna hurt me again! Keep her away from me!"

The nurse helps Aisha out of the room. Miss Lewis stares at a shocked Grace. "How could leave her alone?"

Grace is speechless.

Outside Grace's office, Mrs. Gordon is hollering at the secretary. "Where's my Aisha at? What's goin' on here?" Grace enters, followed by Mrs. Thompson. Mrs. Gordon turns to Grace. "Oh, it's you, Missus Preachie. Gonna save the world, gonna save mah Aisha! You wanna tell me wass goin' on?"

"Not really," Grace mutters.

"I'm tihed a' comin' ta dis fuckin' school. Eitha you gimme mah daughta, o' tell me what you're gonna do 'bout keepin' me on mah couch."

"If you weren't such a stupid, lazy cow, we wouldn't be having this conversation!" Grace goes into her office and slams the door. Mrs. Gordon stands with her mouth gaping open.

Mrs. Thompson quickly interjects, "Mrs. Gordon, please come with me." She guides her by the arm out of the office.

Grace's back is against the slammed door, breathing heavy. She tries to collect her mile-a-minute thoughts. She scrambles to the phone on her desk and dials.

Robert is at his desk and picks up the phone on the first ring. "Hello, my love! Looks like I'll be wrapping up same time. How's the day?"

Grace stutters, "I'm having some problems with... Oh, you know what, forget it. I think I'll cook. You want steak?"

"Perfect. Rare."

"I thought you liked it well done?"

"You know I love you, right? Grace?"

Grace's eyebrows furrow. "I love you too, Robert. Okay, see you later. Can't wait," she says, barely audible, "to see you. Keep it up." She hangs up the phone. There is a sharp knock on her door, causing her head to snap.

Miss Lewis barges in, seething. "How dare you!"

Grace is quick to compose herself. "What is it, Miss Lewis?"

"I don't know what your problem with me is..."

"Oh, don't you?"

"But to take it out on one of my students is too much."

"What are you insinuating, Miss Lewis? I have enough to deal with." Grace begins shuffling papers on her desk.

"I'm referring to Aisha. Right now she is in the nurse's office, crawled up in a ball, hysterical crying. She said you called her an animal."

"You know very well the girl is emotionally unstable and a danger to herself and others. I've done all I can do for her. Her mother is here to pick her up. Expulsion effective immediately."

"I don't know what's happened to you, Grace. All of a sudden you decide to give up on her? We've been making progress, now you want to throw it all away? What, your husband's new money has got you confused with what's important around here?"

"You make another comment like that, and you'll be the next to go home. I saw the way you looked Robert. You want what I have, that's obvious. Jealousy doesn't suit you. Now, get back to your class."

"Don't be so sure of that husband of yours."

"What does that mean?"

"Have a nice day, Grace," Miss Lewis turns quickly, and walks out.

Grace picks up the phone, blocks caller ID, and dials.

Robert answers quickly, "Nash Rice... Hello? I don't have time for this shit..."

Grace hangs up and stares straight ahead.

Miss Lewis is holding Aisha's hand. They are standing at the door as Aisha's mother gathers her things. The rest of the class is working on an assignment, glancing up occasionally to stare at Aisha and her mother. Grace enters the room.

"Okay, class. Please place your papers on my desk and line up quietly for gym," Miss Lewis says. She bends down and addresses the little girl. "Good-bye, Aisha." Miss Lewis gives her a kiss on the cheek.

Aisha, seeing Grace, grabs Miss Lewis around the neck and hugs her tightly. Mrs. Gordon takes her daughter by the hand. "Mama, Mrs. Rice is mean. She said she was gonna punch me in de fuckin' face!"

"You said that to ma daughta'? I'm gonna repote you to the Board a Ed. This ain't ova yet!" They make their way out of the classroom.

"Ok, papers please," Miss Lewis addresses her class. Nobody moves. Grace scoffs and walks off.

Miss Lewis sits with her lunch in the teacher's lounge. Mr. Connor enters and takes a seat next to her, "Hey, how's it going?"

"Haven't you heard? Mrs. Rice lost her shit. She threatened one of my students, potentially harmed her, then expelled her."

"Now that's something to tell the guy from the Board of Education."

"Which guy?"

"That one that was flirting with you last week."

"That was Mrs. Rice's husband!"

"What? He told me he was working for the district. Whoa, now you know why she's giving you such a hard time."

"What exactly did I do?"

"Not what you did. There's obvious dysfunction in her marriage right now. And it's effecting her work."

"Maybe she needs a lesson in humility."

"You got that right," Mr. Connor mumbles, returning to his coffee and paper grading. Miss Lewis takes a bite of her sandwich, an idea forming. She rummages through her bag and finds the piece of paper that Robert gave her with the address for O'Henry's.

The bell rings and children run out of the school, towards their buses.

As Grace is grabbing her suit jacket and briefcase, Mrs. Thompson pokes her head in. "Grace, you ok?"

"Fine. Why?"

"I guess I should tell you, because I'm the only one who would. But it's not good."

"What?"

"There's a rumor going around, about your husband and Miss Lewis. And I'm only telling you because you're my friend."

"What's being said? "

"That they're having an affair."

"Godamnit!" Grace runs passed Mrs. Thompson, and down the hall. Grace races to Miss Lewis's classroom and throws the door open only to find a lone custodian emptying the trash. Grace slams the door several times until the window in the door breaks.

Miss Lewis is speeding along the highway, as traffic leaving the city fills the opposite lane.

Robert sits on a stool at O'Henry's, shot in one hand, cigarette in the other. The brokers surrounding him tell jokes and laugh. Robert's cell phone rings. He takes it out of his pocket, sees the number, and pushes END. He sets the phone down on the bar and continues drinking, lost in thought.

Grace hangs up the phone, frustrated, and enters a nail salon, slamming her briefcase down in front of a startled manicurist. She sits down heavily and pulls up her sleeves, as the manicurist begins taking polish off of her nails. After a short minute, she throws her hands in the air, takes a twenty from her wallet, and throws it down on the table. She exits in a hurry and heads home.

Miss Lewis enters O'Henry's and searches for Robert. She sees him and slowly saunters over to his group. Sal and Brian Beckerman flank Robert on either side, fighting to get his ear next.

"Listen, man, I got some incredible new hookers. They're like eighteen-year old models. You won't believe it. Two grand a piece, but you get 'em all night. These girls must've learned from Daddy at age twelve, 'cause they really know what the fuck they're doing," Sal yells over the music.

Miss Lewis taps Robert on the shoulder. He turns, pleasantly surprised. "Hey! Miss Lewis, how ya doin', doll? Beckerman, get up and give the lady your seat. Come on, move move move." Beckerman gets up and offers Miss Lewis the stool. Robert turns to the bartender, "Hey, Mario! Give her whatever she wants."

Sal continues his attempt to stir up some fun. "There shouldn't even be a conversation right now. These girls will let you do whatever you want to 'em. Come on, let's go. They're going to be at my apartment in an hour. We'll call in an eight ball and have a party with some barely legals. What's better than that?"

Miss Lewis notices a phone on the bar ringing. "Nash, is this your phone? It's ringing," she says, touching his arm.

"Don't worry about it," he says. He turns to Sal. "I'd like to thank you."

"For what?"

"The hookup at the Bellagio. I can't even tell you. The room? Windows overlooked the entire city. The service was first class."

"I told you I had the hookup!"

Miss Lewis is staring at Robert's phone. The caller ID reads HOME. She watches as it continues to ring.

Grace hangs up the phone and then redials. She is mumbling to herself, with tears in her eyes. She slams the phone down, takes the steak out of the refrigerator, and sticks it on a platter, raw. She carries it to the dining room table that is set for two and sticks a large, two-tine carving fork in it.

"Me and my wife got back to the room after a night of decadence, I looked at her and I wanted to cry. She took off all her clothes, put her hands on the window, and looked out onto the city. I came up behind her and had my arms around her, and it gave me the most incredible feeling. I'd rather go home and eat steaks with her than get my dick muddied."

"I'd call you whipped, but I want to stay on your good side," Sal says.

Miss Lewis sees the phone ring again. She reaches over and presses the TALK button. "Nash, pay attention to me," she purrs.

"You know, I never did get your first name. I don't even want to know. I just want you as Miss Lewis. Hey Sal, get over here. This is Miss Lewis."

"Nice to meet you," he says, turning back to Robert. "I don't want to keep those girls waiting."

"Nah, you're missing it. Miss Lewis is a schoolteacher. Come on, Sal. A schoolteacher! Trust me, it's better to fuck the teacher than the students. The teacher knows best. I mean look, Sal, she's got the nicest ass. Think of the fantasies. I've already had them."

Miss Lewis offers her best doe eyes. "But Nash, you know I came here to see you. All your sweet talk in the teacher's lounge the other day really got me going."

"I'd love to, but I gotta get outta here."

"You made me come all the way down here for nothing? Shame on you!"

"Alright, sweetheart. Hey, Mario! Give us another round!" Miss Lewis hears screaming through the phone. She reaches behind Robert's back and pushes END on his cell phone. She turns the phone off and slips it into her bag.

Grace is unraveling. "You son of a bitch! How could you fucking do this to me!" she screams and, upon hearing the call disconnect, she impulsively throws the phone across the room. Grabbing the nearest objects off the counter, mainly dishware, she takes out her rage by smashing things to the floor. She manages to break everything within her reach, her tears starting and stopping with unusual celerity. She slowly takes a seat at the kitchen table, dazed.

The party is in full swing. Mario does his best to replace the empty shot glasses with new ones as fast as he can. Miss Lewis dances with Rosenshwag, extending her arms out to Robert to encourage him to cut in. Rosenshwag is busy sneaking squeezes wherever he can land, Miss Lewis slapping his hand each time and cracking Robert up. He casually looks down at his watch and jumps off his stool. "Oh shit!" he utters and heads for the door.

"Nash, where are you going?" Miss Lewis calls after him.

He calls out behind him, "Hey, Rosenshwag. Take care of the teacher. I'm going home to my wife."

Robert exits quickly. Rosenshwag continues drunkenly groping a miserable looking Miss Lewis.

Robert drives at an even pace wearing a content demeanor, his music choice soothing. He pulls quietly into the driveway and notices the lights are out in the entire house, the windows dark. He gets out of the car, hearing the sound of insects getting louder with each step. He looks around, up and down the block, and sees nothing unusual. The sound is coming from the house and is growing in fever and pitch. He runs toward the house, fumbling with his keys, and unlocks the front door. He lets himself in, the door slamming behind him.

Robert moves through the darkened house, first turning on the hallway light and then the kitchen, exposing the broken glass chaos. "Grace?" He takes the stairs two at a time.

Grace stands at the end of the dark hallway, her silhouette illuminated but for the light from below. She holds her arms out straight, pointing the gun he had stashed in his safe directly at his heart.

"Grace, what are you doing," he whispers.

"Don't talk to me. Don't you say another fucking word to me," her voice flat and dreary as melted asphalt.

"Why are you turning on me?"

"You fucking cheat on me and then make me the bad guy? That's low, even for you."

"Where is this coming from? I haven't cheated!"

"I can't take another lie. There's nothing left."

"I love you, Grace. Don't do this. I'm going to hell no matter what. Do you want to join me?"

"I'm already there," Grace says coolly and shoots him, twice, in the chest.

He falls back and hits the floor, choking on his own blood. He cries out in a voice that is small and timid. And familiar. "Gracie, what did you do?"

She falls to her knees next to him. The phone rings. She gets up and walks towards the darkened bedroom, and picks up the receiver by the bed. "Hello?" she croaks, barely able to produce sound.

"Grace? It's me. I'm sorry to call you at your house so late, but I thought that you should know. Tonight I did something very spiteful, which is not in my nature. I went to see your husband at the bar where he drinks after work. I tried to seduce him, to hurt you the way you hurt me by undermining my work. I realize now how foolish it was, to do something so childish. Maybe my students are starting to rub off on me a little. Anyway, I wanted to apologize. Your husband loves you so much and I thought you should know that."

Grace drops the phone on the receiver and walks back over to Robert. She puts her head on his stomach and wraps his lifeless arms around her. She takes the gun and puts it into her mouth. She squeezes the trigger.

VIII

A bitter wind howls above the huddled sots in their ragged coats as they hurry through the dark streets, avoiding contact. There are no holidays here, no rest from the incessant misery that gauges time eternal.

Nash blasts past them, running at top speed. He hears a grating cackle and spots a black prostitute in a tight red dress, cleavage spilling out. She is pointing at

86

Nash and laughing at him. "You think it's forever! But it ain't! I sure got her with them gerbils, tho, dint I?"

Nash continues through the street, calling out, "Grace! Grace!"

Voices from the shadows mock him, "Grace! Grace! Grace!"

He kicks down the front door of one tenement building to the next, hollering into empty corridors. From far off, he hears muffled screams and follows the sound. In the living area of one complex, a feast is taking place, skin on skin, as a group of men devour a woman with their sex. Nash charges in and peels them off of her, a rusty old swine cursing him with her boiled skin and rotten teeth, "This is how I like it, you freak! Get the hell outta here!" She throws her shoe at him while the others look on dumbly, cocks in hand.

Nash continues filling the streets with her name, his anxiety growing. From a boarded up, rundown flat a tiny voice pings his eardrum. "Nash? Is that you?"

Nash races over to the flat and peels off the insecure plywood board covering the door, climbing through. He makes his way down a dark hallway and enters a dusty room empty of furniture shy one lone chair. Grace is huddled on it, her sobs buried in her knees as she clutches them to her chest. "Grace!"

Grace looks up, confused. She stares at his unfamiliar face recognizing the look in his eyes. "Nash?" she chokes out a crazy kind of laugh and slowly stands. He runs towards her. They embrace, never to let go.

X X X

Bar None is aglow with red lighting, acid-jazz music spilling outside the heavily guarded front door. The Devil walks up to the bouncers in a sharp suit, his long curly hair slicked back, a cigarette dangling from his delicate fingers. "Good evening, gentlemen. I believe I'm on the list."

"Right this way, Sir," the first bouncer hurries to usher the guest of honor inside. Red velvet still blankets the walls, but now there are fine works of art hanging from them and the dark wood of the bar is expertly polished. Behind it, Ricardo wears a black bowtie and pours tall, bottomless drinks. Upon seeing the Devil, he greets him warmly and signals to Nash.

Pushing through the crowd of happily drunk people, Nash holds up his arms in a celebratory fashion. "Welcome! Glad you could make it," Nash beams. Grace appears from behind him donning an exquisite vintage dress, her hair and makeup impeccable.

"Grace, you are ravishing," the Devil says, gently taking her extended hand and kissing it.

"It's surprising how comfortable I feel," she smiles easily, swaying to the music.

"Not so surprising you belong here, darling woman, as this place was designed for the wicked. You are most welcome as one of those for whom hell has the chance to thrive. Here, the fear of aging and death has been removed. Here, you have all that you desire, found merely in the act of desiring of it. Here, sin is virtuous!"

The music stops as Nash takes to the newly built stage. "Ladies and Gents, I'd like to thank you for coming tonight. We have a special treat in store for you. But before we get to it, I'd like to personally thank the Devil for bringing me together with my true love. Without her, well, this place would really be Hell!" The audience laughs. He continues, "Grace, we make the best of one another, and for that I'm eternally grateful. Literally!" There is more laughter mixed with jeers. "Ok, enough sap. Please put your hands together for Buzzy Klein!" Nash exits the stage and takes his place next to his lady.

As the applause subsides, the curtain opens to an enormous, bald body builder standing center stage, wearing a dark blue singlet, his skin stretched painfully over muscles covering his entire body. Surrounding him are women in various degrees of undress, lounging languidly about the stage. It's a Man's World begins to play, as the muscle man hoists an impossibly large barbell over his head with ease. The women look away seemingly unimpressed. The music continues as the man continues to stand there, flexing his already swollen biceps. The song ends and he grabs the edge of his singlet and rips it off, revealing a hairless pussy between his legs. The audience goes wild.

Grace tugs on Nash's arm. "Oh my! My love, who is that?"

"Buzzy Klein. Murdered eighteen women in the seventies. Became a very well known porn star before they caught up with him. Or her."

"Bizarre!" she laughs.

"I adore you," he smiles and kisses her gently. As the party takes off, people dancing gently to the music around them, they are the only two people in the room that matter, forever.